ABOUT THIS BOOK

Welcome to Havenwood Falls, a small town in the majestic mountains of Colorado. A town where legacies began centuries ago, bloodlines run deep, and dark secrets abound. A town where nobody is what you think, where truths pose as lies, and where myths blend with reality. A place where everyone has a story. Including the high schoolers. This is only but one . . .

Two houses. Two hearts. One fate.

Growing up in the prestigious Fairchild house seems like the perfect life, but for Julianna, it isn't always easy, especially as the granddaughter of a prominent Seelie Court elder. When Julianna's grandfather passes away, her parents are summoned to the fae island of Tír na nÓg. Not wanting to miss her senior year of high school, Julianna decides to remain in Havenwood Falls with her human grandmother, unaware this one choice will forever change her perfectly planned future.

Lies, secrets, and betrayals rule in the Bishop house, and Rowan Bishop, the youngest of the brothers, is no exception. Unpredictable and uncontrollable, he's been kicked out of eight private boarding schools. As a last-ditch effort to set him straight, his oldest brother enrolls him in Havenwood Falls' Sun and Moon Academy—a private school for residents with supernatural gifts.

After several chance encounters, Julianna and Rowan discover a connection full of attraction, mystery, and danger. A connection that lands them right in the middle of a centuries-old feud between the Bishops and the Fairchilds. And when it comes to choosing sides, the cost of their forbidden love will be higher than they ever expected.

INAMORATA

A HAVENWOOD FALLS HIGH NOVELLA

RANDI COOLEY WILSON

HAVENWOOD FALLS HIGH BOOKS

Written in the Stars by Kallie Ross
Reawakened by Morgan Wylie
The Fall by Kristen Yard
Somewhere Within by Amy Hale
Awaken the Soul by Michele G. Miller
Bound by Shadows by Cameo Renae
Inamorata by Randi Cooley Wilson
Fata Morgana by E.J. Fechenda (March 2018)
Forever Emeline by Katie M. John (April 2018)

More books releasing on a monthly basis.

Stay up to date at www.HavenwoodFalls.com

To Maddison,
Believe in Magic. Believe in Love. Believe in Yourself.

Don't waste your love on somebody who doesn't value it.

~ Unknown

CHAPTER 1

*W*ith blurry vision and bumbling fingers, I grab the buzzing cell phone off the nightstand and glance at the screen. A groan escapes me when my best friend Zaltana's name flashes. Reluctantly, I sit up and wipe the fatigue from my eyes. The phone vibrates again, her ringtone feeling as though it's becoming more annoyed at me with each passing moment I ignore it.

It's a well-known fact that waking me up before dawn never leads to a positive outcome—I am a seventeen-year-old girl who needs sleep. The phone begins to vibrate again, and I end the internal war I'm having with myself whether or not I should answer. It's futile. The guilt has already set in.

"It's two o'clock in the morning," I mumble through a yawn.

"Oh good, you're awake," Zal's overexcited voice replies.

"I am now. What's up?"

A long pause ensues before she answers me. "I need a favor, Jules."

With a low growl, my head falls back onto my pillow. Zaltana Purser always needs a favor.

"What kind of favor?" I try to focus on her words instead of her bubbly excitement.

"Well . . ." she begins in a singsong. "There is this . . . event going on, and I need you to come."

"What kind of event?"

"A. Um. *Sporting* event." Her reply is vague.

I stifle another yawn. "At this hour?"

"I know. I know. You need your beauty sleep. The cool part is they needed a healer last minute, and River recommended me." Her grin is clear in her voice as she talks about her crush.

"The favor?" I prompt.

"I need a ride home. River went missing, and it's almost over."

My gaze wanders to the alarm clock. It is so freaking late. I sigh, knowing how important this is to her. Zaltana is a Native American medicine healer, a descendant of Chief Aquakawwa. Her grandfather, Chief Joseph Purser, is the current leader of the local band of the Ute Tribe. Since she's seventeen, the elders only allow her to use her powers on the reservation in limited and monitored situations. She wants to make her grandfather proud and honor their tribal legacy, though, so she jumps at any chance to practice and use her gifts wherever and whenever.

"Please, Julianna," she whines. "I wouldn't ask if this wasn't important. You're my best friend. Don't leave me stranded with a bunch of high school seniors."

"We're high school seniors," I remind her.

"What if my powers go all haywire, and I accidentally kill a vampire?"

I cringe. She has a point. Zal isn't the most predictable with her healing abilities.

"Fine," I groan. "Where do I need to meet you?"

She breathes a sigh of relief. "Mount Alexa. Midway up."

"North of town?" I whine. "You're lucky I live in the Heights now."

"My firstborn is yours. Oh, and wear something cute." She hangs up.

Wear something cute? I stare at the ceiling of my new bedroom, wishing everything I'd brought with me was already organized so I could get dressed faster. I sigh, my gaze floating around. Maybe I should have let my grandmother's staff unpack for me when I first moved in and she made the offer, but the thought of strangers touching my things, my books, my clothes—it makes my stomach churn.

I hate the idea almost as much as I hate being here. *Ten months. That's all.*

Tossing my covers off, I force my body out of the comfort of my bed and place my feet on the soft, plush carpet before turning on the dim white twinkle lights surrounding my bedroom.

I've been at the House of Fairchild for a few days, and there is still so much left to do before school starts on Monday. I frown, looking around. With all the cliché antique-white furniture and pink flowers decorating this room, you'd think I was a Disney princess instead of the daughter of a notable Seelie fae. One who is about to take his seat on the Seelie Court.

I miss my parents. Our home. I like routine; I like predictability; I like organization. I hate clutter and messes. And, right now, my predictable, carefully planned-out life in the small town of Havenwood Falls, Colorado—where I've spent my entire life—is full of chaos and disorder. Everything had been perfect, until it all fell apart when my grandfather died.

My fingers twitch with the urge to use my fae powers to fix the clutter, but I ignore my inner voice and let the unpacked boxes stay where they are. What's one more day at this point?

Plus, using my powers in my grandmother's house is a definite no-no. My grandmother, Miss Mary Beth Fairchild, is a human. She becomes anxious when I use my gifts for trivial matters—like cleaning or unpacking boxes. As the matriarch of one of the town's notable families, she likes to remain in good standing with the town's Court of the Sun and the Moon, which oversees all things supernatural. A use of power by an underage fae is not something the Court encourages.

I blink slowly, ignoring my littered surroundings, and attempt to calm the fae energy that flows through me. In January, I turned seventeen and went through my "awakening," coming into my full fae gifts. Since then, I've been practicing with my parents to hone and fine-tune my abilities. I guess all of that will have to be put on hold, now that they were called away.

Both my father and mother are very powerful and highly respected Daoine Sidhe Fae, which means in the Seelie realm that we're royalty. It also means that once my father is permanently appointed on the Seelie Court, I will see even less of my parents than I do now.

My grandfather, Akeel, held a prestigious position on the Seelie Court. When he died in December, he left his seat open. In the fae realm, only a direct bloodline descendant can fill a Seelie Court position after the rare death of an elder. So my father was invited to the island of Tír na nÓg in the fae realm, which required an extended stay for he and my mother to prepare my father to take over my grandfather's position. We've summered on the magical island since I was a small child.

It's the one place I feel free.

Normal.

Where I don't have to hide who and what I truly am.

Unlike this small town I've grown up in.

Forced to mask my true identity from the human residents who call Havenwood Falls home.

That is how I ended up living with my human grandmother, Miss Mary Beth Fairchild. I moved in with her so I could finish out my senior year at Havenwood Falls High School. I stare at the mess, wondering how to best curb my desire to fix it. Even with the handful of items I brought from my parents' house in Creekwood Estates to my grandmother's house in the prestigious Havenwood Heights, it feels like I've moved my entire life.

Getting up, I internally curse Zal as I walk over to my closet, pull out a pair of ripped and washed-out gray skinny jeans, a white tank, and my worn-out black short boots. While brushing my teeth, I debate whether I should try to tame my mass of unruly, long lavender waves. After a few seconds, I throw them into my signature loose side-braid, using my flower hair tie.

Stifling a yawn, I grab my sweater, stuff cash into my pocket, snatch up my car keys and head out, leaving my grandmother a note in the event she wakes up to find me gone.

Seconds later, I am in my Rubicon, heading up to Mount Alexa. Unsure of where to go, I keep my eyes open. Halfway up the mountain I spot the bikes and know I've found the place. *Really, Zal?*

Dirt bikes and motorcycles are parked by the side of the mountain paths, an occasional truck or car between them. A small handful of supernatural students walk around, inspecting them. The riders are all high-school-aged, decked out in ripped jeans and leather jackets, laughing and hanging around with pride-filled grins that ooze confidence. The purring of a few of the bikes gliding over dirt, jumping across rocks, and climbing up the mountain fills the late evening air.

I park my car, shutting it off before hopping out. Instantly, I hear my name, and look over to see my best friend waving her arms over her head. I cross mine over my stomach for warmth as I make my way toward her. Even though it's the end of August, the Colorado air is chilled due to the late hour. The higher up the mountains you go, the colder the air, no matter what season, even now at the end of summer.

"Hey, thanks for coming."

"What is all this?" I ask Zal, staring into her warm brown eyes.

"Motorcycle trials and racing." She beams with excitement.

Her expression falls when she notices the tightness of my lips and the worry in my eyes.

"This is why you dragged me out of bed in the middle of the night?"

"Yes," she replies with a frown. "They needed a healer in case anyone gets hurt."

"In case?" I look around. "Who organized this?"

"River's new friend. He's attending Sun and Moon Academy this year."

At her reply, I realize there are very few kids here from Havenwood Falls High, the public school.

The sound of dirt bikes rumbling cuts off my thoughts as two bikers race down the mountain at insane speeds. I stiffen when the racers barely miss the trees and rock formations surrounding the tight dark path.

"You know this is illegal, right?" I turn to Zal. "If Sheriff Kasun finds out . . ."

"Relax." She waves me off. "It's the last weekend before school. Have some fun!"

I look at her in disbelief. "Fun, huh?"

"Yes. Fun. You remember what fun is, don't you?" Zal pins me with a look.

Feeling a twinge of annoyance, I look away from her, down the path a bit to my right.

A tall, muscular guy is holding a helmet in one hand while he flirts with a group of girls surrounding him. Somehow, he seems older than all the other people milling around. His dirty-blond hair is shorter on the sides and back. The top is shaggy. The relaxed look makes me feel like the style takes more effort to create than it looks like. I roll my eyes. Why do guys do that?

The girls surrounding him giggle and swoon, which makes me assume he's charming, with seemingly little effort. In the moonlight, I notice his face has a perfect symmetry to it. His jawline, a bit of scruff. A headlight beam flashes over him, glinting off his brow and lip piercings. As if he can feel my gaze on him, he turns his eyes my way.

Our gazes meet and lock. I'm instantly captivated, helpless to turn away. There is something carnal about him. Dangerous. Exotic. I stare into his dark-colored eyes as they bore into mine.

One edge of his lips curves into a devilish crooked grin. It's both playful and promising.

"Jules?" Zal's voice breaks the hold he has on me.

Quickly, I turn around so my back is to him and face my friend. Inhaling a deep breath, I attempt to force my heartrate to slow down and my lungs to breathe normally. I'm a hot mess.

"What?" I attempt to keep my voice even.

"The final race is about to start." She grabs my wrist and pulls me up the mountain, so we're closer to the path. As she does, I risk a glance over my shoulder at the hot guy, but he's gone.

Excitement rolls through the small crowd, the energy of the spectators causing a zing of anticipation and excitement to rush through me. With the roar of the bikes, we look up toward the top of the mountain, and my heart stops. Straddling his motorcycle is the hot guy. His helmet is on, but his visor is open. Revving his engine, he looks at me. When our eyes meet, he winks and slams his visor shut.

My pulse quickens as the riders move into position, and with a cheer of encouragement, the starter waves the flags. The bikes surge forward, and I hold my breath, watching as they fight to reach the finish line first. The bikes fly by us in a blur, dodging obstacles by jumping on and off rocks, and fishtailing dirt into the air around corners. It's so dangerous and yet, exhilarating.

Suddenly, the crowd erupts in hoots and hollers, shouting, "Row."

I bend forward and look down the end of the path to see that the hot guy won.

"OMG! That was so awesome," Zal screeches next to me. "Aren't you happy you're here?"

"Thrilled." I exhale my nervousness. "Can we go now?"

She rolls her eyes at me and nods. "Let me just grab my stuff."

"I'll meet you by my Jeep." I turn on my heel and start toward my car.

When I'm within two steps of it, the roar of a bike engine approaches, and the hot guy pulls up between me and my beloved vehicle. The world shifts as I snap my attention to him.

His helmet is off, and his dirty-blond hair is sweaty. The strands stick out messily in a way that makes me want to run my fingers through it. Fix it. Make it perfect. Less . . . wild.

He hunches over his bike, hands on the grip and throttle, while I stare. His penetrating gaze studies my face for a moment. There is something in his eyes I can't quite grasp. It's like a combination of interest and curiosity. And it has me frozen.

His gaze drops and then roams over me—I become helpless and trapped. I note his thick, sooty lashes fanning the tops of his cheeks. When his eyes finally travel north again, he extends his hand toward me, and when he does, my fingers itch to touch him. I don't.

As a headlight from a dirt bike flashes over me, a shadow flickers over his face, darkening his eyes. "Your eyes are violet," he points out.

I nod. Most residents of Havenwood Falls ignore their color. It's normal here. "I know."

As if encouraging me, his grin turns suggestive. "Did you enjoy the race?"

He slouches on the bike, cool eyes holding my steady gaze, as the corners of his mouth tilt up. My heart fumbles a beat, rendering me speechless, as I gawk at him. His smirk isn't welcoming. It reeks of trouble and mischief.

The wind shifts, blowing his scent over me. Looking down, I wrinkle my nose, taking in a deep breath, trying to figure out what he smells like. Something rich and warm. Like hot chocolate mixed with cinnamon buns. Something you to want to curl up with and never let go.

He cocks a brow. "Do you speak?"

For some reason, it doesn't sound as though he is asking me a question. "Of course, I speak."

Something glitters in his eyes. Amusement. "Is it me that you aren't a fan of, or motorcycles?"

I glance up in time to catch another dark grin, this one daring me to answer him, causing me to fall speechless again. Both eyebrows are raised, as if he is questioning my ability to truly speak.

His eyes stay connected to mine. "Nah, it's not me. You're scared of what you can't control."

The sudden need to defend myself claws at my skin.

Who is this guy, and why is he assessing me? Embarrassment and anger fill me at what he's implying. Regardless if he's right or not, he's irritating.

In my group of friends, I'm not the quiet one, but I am focused. On my future. I maintain a perfect GPA, enjoy community service, am captain of the tennis team, and try to be the perfect all-around kid. I'm afraid to do anything reckless or wild; growing up, it wasn't allowed.

I need to find my voice, which is always strong. Right now, I'm just standing here, looking like I don't know how to open my mouth. Or speak. I want to die. *Say something smart, Jules.*

"I'm guessing *fun* isn't in your vocabulary," he challenges.

I take in a deep breath. "This has been a stimulating conversation. One that I will cherish for a long time, but I have to go," I bite out through a tight jaw, and step around him toward my car.

A warm hand snaps out, and long fingers wrap around my wrist, forcing me to stop and whip around, turning my attention to him. At his touch, energy flows between us. He lets out an irritated breath as he stares at the spot we are touching, quickly and almost angrily releasing me.

"You're too tightly wound." His voice is deep and mocking. "With you, it's all about order, control. I bet you have your whole life planned out. Ivy League. Daddy's girl. Flannel pajamas."

"I do not wear flannel pajamas," I lie.

He laughs, deep and throaty. "Naked it is then."

I flip him off. I have no idea why. He's just so infuriating.

He laughs again. "Very civilized."

"Listen . . ." I pause.

"Rowan," he interjects, catching on to the fact I was searching for his name.

My eyes narrow. "Listen, Rowan." His name falls out of my mouth more severely than I intend, but I can't stop myself. "It's clear that most of these airheads find you charming. I don't."

"You sure about that, flannels?"

I smile sweetly. "Oh yeah. Very sure."

"Hey, Bishop." River runs over to us. "You left your helmet at the bottom of the mountain."

Bishop. My heart sinks, and any fantasies I had about him being hot disappear.

"Hey, Jules." River smiles down at me. "I see you met my bud, Rowan Bishop."

"Rowan Bishop?" I repeat in a whisper.

"In the flesh." Rowan winks at me.

"Sorry. I thought you two formally met," River scrambles. "Rowan, this is Julianna."

"Fairchild," I add and watch as Rowan's face falls and realization sets in.

A Bishop and a Fairchild.

Mortal enemies.

No wonder I think he's a douchebag.

He is.

CHAPTER 2

I slide into the booth at Napoli's, and Zal gives me a sheepish grin. Exhausted, I drop my forehead to my arms. The smell of melted cheese, garlic, and roasted tomatoes permeates the air around me.

Without us having to order, Zara walks over to the table and places down our usual—a large cheese pizza and two waters—before dropping the napkins down and leaving my best friend and me to inhale it. Like she does every time we come in here. I love that Zara knows us so well.

Zaltana pulls off a slice and slides it on a plate toward me.

I sit up and frown when I notice her staring at her phone instead of eating.

"Is it just me, or does the cell service in this town blow monkey chunks?" she pouts.

My brows raise. "Expecting a call?"

"Text. Several actually, from River."

I pull off some of the gooey cheese and pop it between my lips before quickly fanning cool air into my mouth.

"Hot," I exhale dramatically when she throws me an irritated expression.

"What are you, four?" she asks on a huff. "We come here at least once a week, and every single time Zara brings us our pizza, you burn your mouth. Wait for it to cool off."

"I can't. I'm starving." I chew and swallow fast so it doesn't burn my throat. "My grandmother's cook uses ingredients like kale and quinoa.

Every morning Chef Anne hands me a green smoothie and tells me that the vitamins and vegetables are good for me." I shiver.

"Well, they are."

My face scrunches. "So are french fries."

She rolls her chocolate eyes. "We've been over this, Jules. Just because they're made from potatoes doesn't mean they count as a healthy vegetable intake."

I press my lips. "So, ketchup . . ."

"Although made from tomatoes, does not count as a daily fruit serving."

"Damn."

"How is it living with Miss Mary Beth?" She smirks, having known my family all her life.

"It's fine. Since she started working for Weston Designs, she's never home."

"Really?"

"Yeah. The library project keeps her busy. I see more of her staff than I do her."

"Well, if I worked for Everett Weston, I'd never be home either," she purrs.

I throw my balled-up napkin at her. "He's completely in love with Graysin. And old."

Zal frowns. "It must have been hard on Miss Mary Beth when your grandfather died."

My gaze slides over her shoulder and focuses on the fire station outside the window.

"All this serious talk is ruining my pizza high." I avoid the topic.

"You look tired. Sleep well?" she teases.

I glare at her. "You know damn well I did not. What possessed you to go last night?"

Her thin shoulder lifts and falls. "I need practice. Plus, River is in this secret society thing. They're the ones who coordinated the race and trials. They tend to do stuff like that, I guess."

"Secret society *thing*?" I parrot.

Her eyes widen, and she leans in, lowering her voice. "Shhh. I wasn't supposed to repeat that."

"Remind me to stop telling you secrets." I throw a pointed glare her way. "Spill. What is it?"

I watch as her eyes dart around guardedly before she leans in. "A secret group at Sun and Moon Academy. I'm not supposed to know about it. Its members and rituals are kept private."

"Then how did you find out?"

"River let some things spill the other night, while we were hot and heavy on his couch."

I scrunch my face at the thought of the two of them lip locking. "Interesting way to get info."

Her eyes twinkle. "Hey. You can't fault me for being good at what I do."

"Obviously."

"Anyway, it's this thing that his new friend, Rowan, introduced River to."

My stomach drops at the reminder of Rowan Bishop. As two founding families of Havenwood Falls, the Fairchild and Bishop houses have been feuding for what feels like ages. A tragic accident started it all, but in recent years, they've blamed one another for anything and everything.

Most recently, my grandmother, who married into the Fairchild name, blamed Roman Bishop, the oldest Bishop brother, for the death of my grandfather—he had a heart attack while arguing with Roman during a private meeting of the Court of the Sun and the Moon. Our families are ongoing mortal enemies.

It's exhausting.

"So, what is going on with you and River?" I ask, trying to steer clear of the topic of Rowan Bishop.

"I dunno. He's hot and cold. One minute, I am the sun and moon. The next, I don't exist."

"It's annoying when they act like that. I mean, do they really think we like it?"

Zal shrugs. "It's cute in the movies, or novels. Just not in real life."

"It's not cute behavior period."

I lift my gaze from my pizza slice and watch her check her cell again, frowning. My best friend is too beautiful and smart to waste her time on someone like River Livingston, III.

In my opinion, most beings pale in comparison to Zaltana's exotic Native American beauty. It draws you in. Even though Zal's personality can be rough around the edges, there's nothing but delicateness in her looks. She fidgets with her dark hair, which is stick-straight and reaches her waist. The raven color pops off her tan skin and nearly perfect features.

Zal has always been tall and thin, even in kindergarten. As we became older, she embraced her height and lanky body, becoming less giraffe-like awkward, and more runway supermodel.

She always highlights her warm eyes by outlining them with turquoise warrior paint. Combined with her makeup, the effect makes her seem more striking. A few girls we go to school with tried to mimic the look last year, only to epically fail.

I watch as she plays with her traditional sterling silver and turquoise necklace. The gift around her neck given to her by the chief is a constant reminder of her place within the tribe.

For me, it would feel like a noose.

For Zal, it's a symbol of pride.

"All right, stop staring at that thing." I pull her focus from her cell.

"Sorry."

"Sounds like you need back-to-school retail therapy."

"Really?" She perks up, finally focusing on me instead of her phone. "But you hate shopping."

"For you," I drop my voice so it sounds dramatic, "I will make this sacrifice."

"See. This is why you are my best friend. The end."

After downing three slices, I throw my napkin onto the table, along with my half of the bill and tip.

"Callie's?" she questions, referring to our favorite store in Havenwood Falls.

"Always."

Callie's Consignments is a popular vintage clothing store in town run by Callie Montgomery. A lot of the high-school kids love her stuff because it's all designer name brands and hard-to-find items. If you love fashion— truly love it—Callie's is a must to shop at. For Zaltana, it's a mecca. For me, it's where I go to distract my best friend from whatever is bothering her on any given day.

After thanking Zara, we leave Napoli's and walk up Eighth Street, toward Main. I take in a deep breath, enjoying the fresh air and afternoon warmth of our last weekend of summer before Zal and I start our senior year. Aside from the fresh Colorado air, there is nothing about this town I am going to miss. Looking around the town center, I remind myself I have just one more year of school, and then I'm off to NYU. Ten months. That is all I have left to endure of this small town before I can be free of it, and all its secrets and restrictions.

Just as we make a left on Main Street, I stop in front of my favorite bookstore, Shelf Indulgence. I stare longingly at the storefront before Zal's sigh pulls me out of my book-haze.

"You have twenty minutes. Meet me at Callie's," she groans, knowing I can easily spend all day in there. Hence the need for the time limit.

"Thanks." I look at her appreciatively before she walks past Coffee Haven toward Callie's.

Once my friend is out of sight, I pull open the door of Shelf Indulgence and step inside. Within seconds, I'm assaulted by the intoxicating smell of books, chocolate, and, oddly, dust.

The chime above me tinkles as the door closes after me. I offer a small smile to Sedona, the owner, who's behind the cash register, surrounded by her popular chocolate cupcakes and cookies.

Since March, I've tended to be a regular in here, ever since our town library burnt down.

Sedona barely looks up from her book to acknowledge me, lost in whatever magical world she's reading about. As I make my way to the back of the store, my fingertips run over the titles she is featuring this month. They're displayed on a round table at the front of the store, along with her book-themed desserts, which are named after the featured books' characters. I walk past her suggestions, ignoring them, and head straight to the classics section. My favorite.

This is where I've spent hours upon hours this summer. Once I'm in the corner, I smile at the shelves and take a moment to appreciate the selection Sedona has amassed.

"Stalking me, flannels?"

Lost in thought, I jump at the deep male voice and drop two of the books I was skimming.

"Crap!" I react quickly, but I'm not fast enough.

Tattooed arms shoot out and grab both books just before they hit the floor. I try not to flinch when my eyes lock with the familiar dark gaze. My throat becomes dry as I glare at the beautiful face, attached to the equally nice body, belonging to the youngest Bishop brother.

Rowan arches a brow, and my insides tighten. "I'd apologize for

14

startling you, but I don't think you'd accept it. And to be honest, I'm not interested in wasting my breath."

"What are you doing here?" Uncomfortable, I look around to see if anyone is watching us.

Rowan's expression morphs into one that screams, *Do I really need to explain?*

This town is full of gossips and busybodies. The last thing I need is for my grandmother to find out, or think, that I was hanging out with Rowan Bishop, or associating with the Bishops.

He grins, noticing my skittishness. "I was going to ask you the same question."

I glance at the shelves hiding us from the rest of the store. My brows pull together, because it seems pretty obvious what I'm doing here, considering the shelves are covered with books and I was just holding and reading two. "It's a bookstore. I am here to buy books," I reply slowly.

Rowan turns his eyes to the bookshelves. "Then, I guess that explains my presence."

Realization sets in that my question was just as dumb as his. Frustrated at the way I become flustered around him, I bite my lip. Never in my life have I disliked someone as much as I dislike Rowan Bishop. Shaking my head, I push away the little voice inside my head asking why.

"I didn't know Bishops knew how to read." As soon as the words leave my mouth, I growl at myself. *What is wrong with me? Could I be any meaner to him for absolutely no reason?*

Curiosity fills his face as he watches me with his intense gaze. He shakes one of the books I was about to drop at me. "Is this what you do with your spare time? Read?" he asks with a teasing tone. "Because I take you more for someone who prefers kicking puppies and kitties."

My mouth falls open in shock. "I am a Seelie fae. We are not cruel to animals."

"Just mages then," he counters.

"Sorry my *hobby* isn't as cool as racing bikes, or lawbreaking, or whatever it is Bishops do."

I reach for the book, but he pulls it away, lifting it so I can't reach it as he takes a step away from me. Rowan's expression turns wolfish, and my stomach does this funny flip-flop thing.

"Let's see, *Romeo and Juliet* and *A Midsummer Night's Dream*." He arches his pierced brow, inspecting the two books I was looking through. "A little cliché, even for a Fairchild. No?"

Angrily, I grab the two books away from him and place them back on the shelf. Even when I have my back to him, there is no ignoring him. I can feel Rowan watching me, my skin tingling under his heavy stare. Composing myself, I turn back to face him. "Shakespeare's writing is timeless, not cliché. I suggest you read some of it before forming an opinion."

Rowan moves closer and leans into my space. "How do you know I haven't read it?"

Attempting to swallow, I try to take a step back, but he pushes closer, trapping me against the bookshelf. He lifts both his arms, caging me in as he stares down into my eyes.

"Just a guess," I whisper.

With a tilt of his head, he smirks. "One story is about forbidden love. The other about lovers controlled by fairies. If you don't see the irony here, flannels, then I can't help you."

I grit my teeth at the strange look on his face as he towers over me. "I don't need your help. What I need is a book for AP English Lit," I whisper.

The intensity in his eyes as they roam over me sends shivers down my arms. "On the contrary, Julianna Fairchild," he coos. "I think you need my help more than you know."

At the sound of my name, my breath catches, and something flickers in his eyes. Rowan's gaze drops to my parted lips. I freeze as he leans closer, his breath caressing my mouth.

A slight noise to our left causes his gaze to narrow, hiding whatever had been there.

As he quickly pushes himself away from me, we both swing our attention to the elderly woman standing at the end of the aisle, Irene Beckett. Otherwise known as the town gossip. Of course, it would be her standing there instead of Sedona. No doubt my grandmother will hear about this.

"I do hope I'm not interrupting anything, Julianna?" She eyes me before focusing on Rowan.

"Not at all, Mrs. Beckett," I stumble. "I was just, um, leaving." I rush the words out as I step away from Rowan's intensity, but his hand darts out and wraps around my wrist, stopping me.

Taking in a sharp breath, I look down at where Rowan is touching me before throwing him an annoyed glance. "Let me go."

His lips twitch. "I'm not sure I can do that, flannels."

My gaze narrows at the nickname, and I stand unmoving. "I have somewhere to be, Rowan."

Mrs. Beckett clears her throat, reminding me she's still here.

"I have to go." I pull out of his grip and rush past Irene, quickly darting into the aisle to the left so I can catch my breath before I leave. *What the hell was all that?* After a moment of collecting myself, I begin to move toward the door, but stop when I hear Irene's cool voice.

"You'd do well to leave her be, Mr. Bishop," she states. "I realize it's been a few years since you've been in town, but surely you remember why you were sent away in the first place."

Curious as to why Rowan left town, I lean closer to the bookshelf to hear.

"I look forward to the daily reminders from you and the other residents of this town," Rowan spits out, before I watch him storm out of the bookstore.

The chime angrily swings back and forth as the door closes behind him.

Stepping back into the aisle so I can't be seen, I watch as Mrs. Beckett makes her way to the cashier desk to pay Sedona for her cookbook, and then leaves. Once she's gone, I step toward the door to leave and meet up with Zaltana at Callie's, but the sound of Sedona's voice has me pausing.

"Jules."

"Yeah?"

"A word of advice—you'll want to be more discreet if you're planning to hang out with a Bishop boy," she warns, without looking up.

"I wasn't planning on hanging out with him," I mumble and push the door open.

"Still," Sedona calls after me, her nose still in the book. "He's here to stay."

And I could have sworn I heard her add "this time" under her breath.

CHAPTER 3

My gaze focuses on the large picture windows as I lie in bed. There is a gentle breeze this morning gliding through the trees outside. The sky is clear, and the air coming through my open windows carries a fresh-cut-grass scent mingled with the aspen trees scattered around my grandmother's expansive property. I inhale, basking in nature. The Seelie fae share a respect for Mother Earth and are very environmentally conscious. We love the outdoors and to be surrounded by forest, which is why my family fell in love with Havenwood Falls. All the trees.

With a final stretch, I roll myself out of bed, grateful to have had yesterday to finish unpacking and organizing. Satisfied with the way my room turned out, I head into the shower before I get dressed and make my way downstairs. Just as I am about to take the final step, something familiar tickles my nose. The warm scent of cinnamon buns.

I head into the kitchen to find Chef Anne fluttering around the stove, dressed in her chef's outfit. Anne has been with my grandmother for ten years. Every Sunday night since I was eleven, my parents and I would attend a formal family dinner here at the House of Fairchild. Chef Anne was always the star of the show. Her quirky personality makes her extremely likable. She is this short round blond woman from "somewhere in middle America," as she likes to say.

Gray eyes swing my way. "Morning, sunshine. Your Nan is in the dining room."

Smiling my thanks, I head down the hall and step into the formal cream-and-gold-decorated room, which overlooks the well-manicured grounds. My grandmother is sipping her tea out of her favorite flower-patterned china at the end of the long table. The *Sun and Moon Tribune* newspaper is splayed out in front of her as she stares absentmindedly into the gardens.

My grandmother is Dame Judi Dench's look-alike. Her short silver hair, deep blue eyes, and five-foot-one height are all the mirror image of the actress. Miss Mary Beth Fairchild even purses her lips like her when displeased. The only difference between the two is Miss Mary Beth lacks the British accent. However, my grandmother's voice is just as deep and formal.

"Good morning, Julianna." Her gaze shifts to me as she lifts her chin.

"Good morning, Gran." I drop a kiss to her cheek before taking the chair next to her.

Just as I finish placing my cloth napkin on my lap, the staff enters the room, led by Michael, the Fairchild house butler. They busy themselves by placing our breakfast plates in front of us, removing the sterling silver covers, and filling our glasses with juice and tea.

"Is there anything else I can get for you, Mrs. Fairchild?" Michael asks.

"No, thank you, Michael. That will be all for now."

"Very well." He tips his head toward her and leads the staff out of the room.

I stare hungrily at the plate filled with an omelet, bacon, hash browns, and a cinnamon bun.

"What? No puke-green vitamin shake this morning?" I tease.

A manicured brow rises at my comment, before my grandmother motions to the plate of fruit between us. "It's your first day back to school, Julianna. Chef Anne suggested your favorites," she replies while spooning her grapefruit. "Did you speak to your mother and father last evening?"

"I did," I answer around a piece of crisp bacon.

"Then you know the Seelie Court has formally approved his appointment?"

"Yup. Dad mentioned it."

An annoyed look is thrown my way at my use of *yup.* My grandmother isn't a fan.

"It's quite a prestigious position. Akeel would be pleased." She trails off for a moment.

"Do you miss him?" I ask quietly.

"Every single day." Her voice is sad. "Now," she rights herself, sitting straighter. "Are you prepared for this academic year? Do you have everything you need?"

"I do. Mom made sure of it before she left."

"It's nice to see she can be useful," she comments, brazenly insulting my mother.

Mom and Miss Mary Beth have a strained relationship, on a good day. It's respectful and cordial, however, my grandmother never felt that my mother was good enough for her only son.

When I was ten, I once overheard my father and grandparents arguing about something my mother did. My father was defending her, but both my grandmother and grandfather were really ticked off. To be honest, I can't even recall what the topic was, though I've always felt it was about me. Just another chapter in the long and sordid Fairchild history filled with drama and social misgivings.

A silence falls between us as we eat breakfast, and my grandmother's focus turns to the *Tribune*. I learned a long time ago not to defend my mother to my grandmother. It's pointless.

"I realize I don't normally work for Everett on Tuesdays and Thursdays. However, since Graysin left town so abruptly, I will need to, just until the library reopens next month. Will you be quite all right for a few weeks with my absence?" she asks, from behind the newspaper.

"School, clubs, and tennis should keep me pretty busy," I mumble.

At the sound of my mumble, the corner of the paper dips and Gran's stern eyes catch mine. "We are on schedule to reopen on Founders Day." She smiles brightly. "Speaking of Founders Day, I was quite pleased to hear that you have been voted Miss Teen Havenwood Falls this year."

"Really?" I exhale and try not to groan at the fact that I won or that she just ruined the surprise, since the winner isn't announced until the ceremony. The only reason I even applied was because my cousin Paisley said it would look good on my college applications.

Gran purses her lips at my lack of excitement. "You aren't pleased? Miss Teen Havenwood Falls is such an honor, Julianna. I'll call Nina at Dress Perfect this week. I am sure she'd be thrilled to design something custom for the occasion that will trigger your excitement."

"Thank you, Gran, but that isn't necessary. I can just see what Callie has for dresses."

"Nonsense. This is a special moment for this family. Nina will create something lovely."

Staring at my empty plate, I concede. The Fairchild name is well known in Havenwood Falls. To look anything less than perfect at a public social engagement is frowned upon. Why argue?

"Sounds good," I reply under my breath.

"One more thing. Before he left, your father arranged for you to attend two evening classes at the Sun and Moon Academy. On Tuesdays at eight, you will attend Fae History. And on Thursdays at eight, you will learn how to hone your gifts during the Awakening Lab. Supplies for both can be picked up this afternoon in the headmaster's office," she explains. "And Julianna, I don't need to remind you that using your supernatural gifts outside of class is not allowed by the Court of the Sun and the Moon. Should you do so, I will revoke your attendance."

"Yes, Gran."

"Good." She puts down her paper and looks at me. "The classes are held later in the evening so it shouldn't affect your academics or your extracurriculars. However, the later hour is not an invitation to get involved with supernatural hoodlum behavior. Are we clear?" She gives me a pointed look.

Hoodlum? "Don't use my powers outside of supernatural school. Got it!"

My grandmother offers me a small, tight smile. "Off you go then. Your senior year awaits."

Relieved I have been dismissed, I stand and give her a quick hug before practically running out of the dining room to meet Zaltana at Coffee Haven—our before-school ritual.

Just as I am about to make my escape, Gran's voice stops me. "Oh, and Julianna."

I turn to face her, and a shadow flickers over her face, darkening her eyes.

"Irene Beckett mentioned you ran into Rowan Bishop yesterday at Shelf Indulgence. I don't need to remind you of the stain the Bishop family is on our community. I also understand Rowan will be attending Sun and Moon Academy this year as a senior. You'd do best to stay away from him. Fairchilds should not be seen consorting with Bishops. It's terrible for our social reputation."

I decide to ignore my inner compulsion to prod her on just why the Bishops are so hated.

Instead, I dip my chin. "That shouldn't be an issue. He seems like a real jerk."

Her face brightens. "The Bishop brothers are known around Havenwood Falls as nothing but trouble. I'm pleased to hear that he repulses you as much as the rest of them do the town."

At her statement, I frown, and my fingers curl into a fist. For some reason, the need to defend Rowan to her surfaces within me. The sunlight coming through the window bounces off the gold wedding band around her ring finger, and my grandfather's face crosses my mind. I nod quickly, reassuring her that I understand, even though I honestly have no idea why they are so hated. The one thing we can both agree on is that I am officially done with Rowan Bishop.

I STARE at the three-story red-brick building for a moment, watching the throngs of human and supernatural students rush through the arched front doors. For the briefest moment, I consider skipping today altogether. Then I remember my perfect attendance record would be tarnished.

Releasing a heavy sigh, I slurp my iced mochaccino, swallowing the final sip, and throw the empty container into the trash as I approach one of the doors. Willow, the owner of Coffee Haven, is my grandfather's cousin, so she hooks me up when I get a craving for caffeine. This morning, though, my cousin Paisley was working because Willow is about to have her baby. Not only did Paisley give me the friends-and-family discount, but she gave me a little something extra, a supernatural boost if you will, because she knows there's no coffee at Miss Mary Beth's, only tea.

And after breakfast with my grandmother this morning, I needed the extra love.

The moment I step into the halls of Havenwood Falls High, I grumble and head to my locker. Another year. The billboards are lined with silver and blue decorations welcoming the students back to school. Our dragon mascot is plastered everywhere. It's nauseating against the cream walls and marbled brown floor.

"Is it me or does Breckin Roberts get hotter every year?" Zal questions, appearing at my side, sucking on her own iced coffee. "We've known him since kindergarten and nothing. Then, boom! He must have taken magic pills this summer, because he looks practically angelic this year."

We watch Breckin walk by us, offering a smile as a form of greeting before I look over at Zal.

I roll my eyes at her, because she is twirling her hair around her finger and staring at his ass.

"It's you," I lie. He's totally hot. "Hey, where'd you run off to after coffee this morning?"

"River," she answers quickly, explaining her disappearance. "Anyway, give me your schedule," she demands, and I hand it over to her so she can see what classes we have together. "Crap. Seriously? We only have lunch together?"

"Really?" I lean over her shoulder and cross-reference the pieces of paper. "Ugh."

She frowns. "It's going to be a long year."

We make our way to my locker, and I grab back my schedule for the combination.

"Senior year morning announcements. Zara is still pretending to be British," Zal whispers.

"Still?" I meet her eyes.

"Yeah, it's kinda funny. Cute. But funny."

"Oh, and while I was at Callie's, I found out she banned Serena Alverson, again."

"Why?"

"Why do you think? The girl hacks up her vintage pieces. You know how Callie is . . . 'Vintage is to be revered and loved. Don't mess with my pieces. If you don't love them, don't buy them,'" she repeats Callie's mottos, mimicking her voice.

"Serena is crazy. She needs to stop pissing off Callie if she wants to keep shopping there. Gypsy-demons can be vicious when provoked." I exhale. "And Callie has an edge to her."

"I forgot, what's your first class?" she asks, leaning on the row of lockers.

"Chemistry," I reply, rolling my eyes as I open my locker, because apparently caffeine makes Zal forgetful, since we just shared schedules, like ten seconds ago.

"I have AP Calc and Chemistry second period."

I nod, already knowing that. "Guess I'll see you at lunch then."

"See ya then." Zal swaggers off.

Just before I'm about to turn my attention back to my locker, Paisley runs by me. She looks stressed, like she's running late, again. Paisley and I are third cousins, we are both seniors, and we have the same deep violet eye color. That is where the similarities end, though. She got lucky and grew up with the *normal* part of the Fairchild family, working with Willow at Coffee Haven. Whereas I got stuck with the part that likes to lock me in the tower.

I turn my attention back to my locker, and my head tilts when I notice a book already sitting inside it. I pinch my brows, confused, because who would have access to my locker or my combo?

"Where did this come from?" I say to myself.

I pull out the leather-bound copy of *Romeo and Juliet,* the same copy from Shelf Indulgence Rowan and I were holding this weekend, and read the handwritten note attached to it.

Believe it or not, Mr. Shakespeare never meant for his plays to simply be read.
He meant for them to be lived in and experienced firsthand.
Wanna live a little, flannels?
-R

Sighing, I place the book, along with a handful of notebooks, into my locker and slam the door shut. For a moment, I just stare at the front of my locker. How the hell did Rowan gain access to it? The school's wards would block any use of his magic on campus. And why is he leaving books in it for me? With a shake of my head, I grab my backpack and sling it over one shoulder before heading to my first class.

So much for being done with Rowan Bishop.

⌒

THE FIRST RULE you learn as a supernatural resident of Havenwood Falls is: protect the secrets. Don't ask me which ones specifically, because this town is laced with them. One being the Sun and Moon Academy—established as a private school for the town's non-human residents.

Tucked away near the waterfalls, the Academy sits hidden behind trees, on acres of perfectly manicured grass and stone pathways. Guarded from humans by stone walls and tall, metal gates, the entire setting screams elitist. Most of the students who study here are considered troubled or they don't have full control over their powers yet. Then, there are those whose highbrow parents love the idea of their offspring receiving the highest level of supernatural education.

The sound of the falls and the mist blowing off them settles around me as I lean against my Jeep, parked in the circular driveway in front of the massive two-story castle-like stone building.

While I wait, I soak up the magical energy coming off the falls, which is the reason the school was placed so close to them. I watch with slight annoyance as the uniformed students stroll in and out of the arched entry leading into the school's interior courtyard.

Ever since I was born, the Fairchild expectation was that someday I would attend the private school; however, my mother insisted that I go to Havenwood Falls High.

She liked the idea of me matriculating with humans.

"Stalking me again, flannels?"

At the sound of Rowan's voice, I stand straighter and watch as he walks toward me.

Rowan Bishop has this powerful presence surrounding him. He moves with a graceful yet deadly swagger that pulls everyone's attention to him like a magnet, especially when he runs his fingers through his tousled hair. His body language screams privilege and control. Like he's the only one in the world that matters. It's off-putting and at the same time, extremely attractive.

And, yes, apparently, I need to get my head checked out.

My gaze falls to his jeans, which hang low on his hips. When he lifts his arm to fix his hair, he flashes golden skin. The movement somehow makes the top of his pants all the more interesting. I narrow my gaze at the relaxed material, wondering how he is getting away with wearing jeans, since everyone else is in khakis.

Lifting my eyes, I take in his untucked, wrinkled, white button-down shirt, which is slightly open at the top, revealing more golden skin. His sleeves are rolled up, showing off his tattoos.

Rowan isn't wearing a tie or crested jacket like everyone else, and for some reason, the idea of him thinking he doesn't have to because he's better than everyone at this school ticks me off.

When he shifts his book bag from one hand to the other, I hastily avert my eyes to the book in my hand. I know he's staring at me, because the entire length of my body tingles.

"You are here for me, right?" His smile is lopsided when I glance up.

It takes me a moment to collect my breath because when the sun hits him, the effect is breathtaking. I feel my cheeks redden at the sparkle in his eyes as he watches me. I was wrong about his eye color. In the sun, they are this beautiful shade of navy. A dark, deep, familiar blue.

We don't look away from one another. We just stay in this epic staredown that I refuse to back down from. Something passes between us, reminiscent of a strange familiarity. An image of two children playing in a field of sunshine runs through my mind, but dissolves quickly.

Eyes still on me, he leans closer, his breath dancing along my cheek. "Julianna?"

"Hm?" I bask in his closeness.

"Do I need to call Sheriff Kasun and get a restraining order?"

His question is like a slap in the face, forcing me to come back to my senses. "What?"

He steps back, and his grin kicks up a notch. "You're stalking and staring at me."

Yes. Yes. I. Am. Who wouldn't? Gah. Look at him. "I am not."

Rowan smiles, and his eyes do that twinkly thing again, causing me to roll mine at him.

"If you say so, flannels."

"I say—" I stop myself. "Here." I shove the book he left in my locker at him. "This is yours."

"Actually, it's yours. A gift."

"I can't accept it, Rowan."

"Why not?"

I throw him a pointed glare. "You know why not."

"Is it because I stole it?" he asks seriously.

My mouth falls open, and I lower my voice, stepping closer. "You stole this book?"

"Would it bother you if I did?"

My eyes dart around. "Sedona is going to be pissed when she finds out. Why would you steal it anyway? From a witch, no less. Your family is wealthy. You can certainly afford to pay for it."

"Extremely wealthy, actually," he corrects with a cocky smirk.

"Then why do you need to steal a twenty-dollar book from Shelf Indulgence?"

"More like two hundred. It's a first edition." He shrugs. "And because . . . I can."

Unsure of how to respond, I just stare at him with my mouth agape. After a few stupefied moments, I regain my composure. "Stealing is illegal, Rowan."

"So is motorcycle racing on the town's mountains, Jules," he replies, and something familiar in me flickers when he says my nickname. "It's never stopped me before."

"You're such a jerk," I exhale.

Rowan shrugs. "I never claimed to be anything else."

I stare at him, and something dawns on me. "You know, I've lived in Havenwood Falls my entire life. Why don't I remember seeing you around town before? I've seen Roman and Ronan."

He smiles sadly. "My brothers were overprotective—baby of the family and all that," he lies. I know this because one of my fae gifts is sensing deceit.

"Try again," I call him out.

"I was homeschooled and wasn't allowed to venture into town much."

"Care to elaborate?"

He clenches his jaw. "I tended to be . . . unruly and unpredictable. Roman thought I might let the town secrets slip. Scare the mortals. Or worse, kill them. My powers are stronger than my brothers', and I came into them earlier than most mages do. Therefore, I was a loose cannon."

My eyes flick to the building behind him. "But now you're allowed to attend?"

"Forced, actually. When I was ten, I was sent away to the boarding schools."

I flick my gaze back to him. "Schools? As in plural?"

"Eight, to be exact." Rowan beams, as if proud.

"Why so many?"

"Human private schools tend to frown upon illegal or immoral behavior."

My eyes widen. "You were kicked out?"

"Excused," he counters.

"How scholarly and responsible of you."

"They're just schools," he argues.

"If someone leaves Havenwood Falls, their memories are wiped."

"Roman stepped in. I was allowed to keep mine," he replies.

"Why?"

"Reasons."

"Reasons?" I look around before meeting his eyes. "You were finally free of this town. And now—"

"Now what?" he cuts me off.

"You're stuck here again," I finish, holding his gaze. *Why do I even care?*

Rowan's features soften. "Maybe here is where I want to be."

My gaze searches his. "Why?" I ask. "What could possibly be of any interest to you here?"

Something shadows his expression before he takes a step away from me. "That," he motions to the book I'm trying to give back to him. "It's yours. A gift from the Order."

Confused, I scrunch my nose. "The what?"

He doesn't answer me, just continues to back away, holding my eyes.

"Rowan," I call out. "Wait," I demand, only to be met with the sound of his laughter, which causes me to stand there, rooted to the ground, the sound rattling my core.

"See you around town, flannels."

CHAPTER 4

idgeting, I stare ahead blankly at the pale pink wall while Zaltana tilts her head and studies me. At her silence, the knots in my stomach tighten even more. I look ridiculous. As soon as I put on the lace-and-satin dress, I knew it. And my best friend's expression is confirmation.

The short, poofy, itchy dress my grandmother had designed for me is way too much. With a growl, I wobble on the obnoxiously high heels and as the layers of tulle under the dress shift, so does my mood. I can't go to Founders Day dressed like this—in front of the entire town. Even worse, I would have to accept a crown, sash, and title dressed like a doll.

Pouting, I blame my cousin for all this insanity and look longingly toward my bed at my jeans and converse sneakers. Paisley talked me into submitting the application for Miss Teen Havenwood Falls. She was getting ready to turn hers in, but was afraid to do it by herself. Begrudgingly, I agreed to submit one with her because, well one, she promised I wouldn't win, and two, she said it would look good on our college applications—since the judges look at grades, community service, and talent. How I won with my lame flute playing I'll never know.

The only good thing about all this is the $2,500 scholarship for college.

And that we all get the day off from school.

"Zal?" I prompt, irritated.

"Shh," she hushes me. "I'm visualizing."

"Visualizing what?"

"You." She pauses, then smirks wickedly. "Falling off the stage and breaking your neck."

Our gazes meet. "They're too high, right?"

"There is no way you can wear that outfit." She laughs. "I love you like a sister, but your ass can't wear those heels, let alone on the grass, in a short skirt. You'll flash the entire town."

"I know," I growl, and she motions for me to get undressed, which I do.

"I'll fix it," she promises and heads into my walk-in closet.

"I can't wait for this school year to be over. I'm ready to get the hell out of this town."

Zal snickers at my rant and searches through my clothes. "Havenwood Falls is the epicenter of small-town weirdness, that's for sure."

My focus slides over to the copy of *Romeo and Juliet* sitting on my vanity, and I scowl at it.

After Rowan's theft admission, I went straight to Sedona at the bookstore and tried to return it, but she swore it had been paid for and wouldn't take it back per her *no return, no refund* policy.

For the past three and a half weeks, it has just been sitting in my room, taunting me. Reminding me that I haven't seen Rowan since our encounter outside Sun and Moon Academy, and for some reason, the idea of not seeing him irks me even more than owning a stolen book. I need professional help.

The longer I stand here thinking about Rowan Bishop, the stupider I feel. Who cares that I haven't seen him? And why am I holding on to the book? I never even wanted it in the first place.

My focus bounces from Zal to the book a few times, before she looks over her shoulder at me. "Here."

She tosses me a dark pair of navy velvet skinny jeans, a navy three-quarter-sleeved top that drapes in the front, and navy heels, which are much shorter than the ones my grandmother chose.

"Better." I smile at her.

"Wear the sneakers to Founders Day. Then switch into the heels before you're announced and have to go onstage." She curtsies at me. "Your Highness. Hey, am I your lady-in-waiting?"

I step out of the heels and make a face at her back before redressing. "Ha. Ha. Very funny."

"I thought so." She faces me and smirks. "Be quick. I want to see if River actually shows up."

Bending down, I slip on my sneakers and tie the laces. "You don't think he will?"

Zal feigns indifference. "I don't know. He said he and Rowan would be there. Who knows?"

That unwanted, weird feeling I get whenever Rowan's name is mentioned appears deep inside me. Standing to my full height, I glance at the expensive lace dress balled up on my bed.

"My grandmother is going to kill me for not wearing that."

"Come on." Zal motions me forward. "She'll get over it."

Determined to give Rowan back the book, I grab it and throw it in my bag. This time, I'm resolved not to take no for an answer. Even if I have to use fae magic to force it down his throat.

We make our way through the sea of residents in the town center getting ready to celebrate. Founders Day is a big deal every September. It's a day of races and competition in the morning, a picnic lunch provided by the Burger Bar in the afternoon, and later on in the evening, residents perform the reenactment of the founding of the town.

That's usually the time when the high school kids leave and head down to the river's edge to hang out with friends. This year, the town library is reopening after the tragic fire in March, which makes today even more special for Havenwood Falls residents.

"There they are, come on." Zal grabs me and drags me toward a group of people our age.

River bows regally at me as we approach, and the group's focus turns to us.

"Sorry, I spilled the beans to him that you'll be crowned later," Zal whispers next to me.

"Well, if it isn't Miss Teen Havenwood Falls herself," River teases me from where he's standing.

I scrunch my nose at his dramatics. "Whatever."

Rowan's eyes meet mine, and I offer him a weak smile.

He doesn't return it, causing me to readjust my gaze to Zaltana, who is chatting and flirting obnoxiously with River, twisting her midnight hair around her fingers as she giggles.

River attended Havenwood Falls High with us until last year, when he turned seventeen and came into his warlock powers. Since he was unable to control them at first, the Court—which oversees the supernatural residents of Havenwood Falls—ordered his parents to send him to Sun and Moon Academy in an effort to help him gain control over his gifts away from the eyes of humans. Zal was heartbroken. She's loved River ever since he pushed her on the playground in kindergarten for taking his soccer ball.

River winks. "Ladies, you know Paisley's friend, Taylor." He motions to the bubbly girl who offers a bright smile and wave. Her long wavy black hair bounces with her. "She attends the Academy with us. And you both know Gallad and Breckin from Havenwood Falls High," he adds. "As well as Torent and Kai." He continues making introductions as Zaltana waves to the group.

My focus shifts back to Rowan, though, tuning out River, because Rowan's arm is draped around Taylor's shoulders. I watch her press her side right up against him, smiling at what Rowan's whispered in her ear. At the sight, my stomach knots as I stand here awkwardly.

"You can't be serious," I whisper under my breath.

Rowan lifts his head from Taylor's ear, and I can feel my cheeks flame with humiliation and embarrassment as my gaze jumps between the two. *Crap.* I didn't mean for that to be heard.

"Actually, this is pretty serious." With a roguish grin, Rowan presses his cheek into Taylor's neck, and suddenly a dark, unwanted feeling of jealousy ignites inside of me. *What the hell?*

I drag my eyes away from them, focusing on Zal. "I have to go."

"Go?" She frowns. "Go where? You have to be on stage later."

"You stay." I motion to River, knowing she wants to. "I'll be back in time."

"That's a good idea," Rowan interjects, and my eyes swing to him.

"Are you sure?" Zal asks quietly next to me, but I don't respond.

The burning sensation in my chest at the way Rowan is looking at me spreads throughout my veins, and I rake my gaze over him, confused at the harshness in his tone and glare. My heart is already pounding in my chest when his eyes meet mine, staring at me through thick lashes.

In the bright sunshine, I can see the devious glint in his eyes, silently challenging me. *What is his deal today? And why the hell does he have to have such incredible eyes?* They're always so intense, like when he looks at you—truly looks at you, like he's looking at me now—nothing else around him matters. The air between us crackles with tension as we stare at one another.

Tearing his gaze from me, he looks at River. "Run along, Your Highness." His words are cold as he directs them at me.

"Screw you, Bishop," I mumble, and both guys twist to look at me. "Why are you even here?"

Rowan's eyes harden as he studies me. "Easy there, flannels. I have just as much right to be here today as you do. Regardless of my last name or who my family is."

For some reason, I feel like his words cover me in a layer of filth, making me sick.

River and Zaltana look confused as their eyes flick between Rowan and me.

With a shake of my head, I step away and throw Zaltana a *see you later* look. Without pause, I start walking toward the library, where I know my grandmother will be. She and Everett's design team are working on last-minute touches before the mayor cuts the ribbon and officially opens the new library to residents later this morning.

A few minutes later, I all but run up the stairs and push open the heavy double-arched doors, entering the quiet building. The new library has an old-world Spanish-Gothic feel to it. It's two stories, open, bright, and airy. The walls are a light cream, with high ceilings and iron-looking chandeliers. Everett Weston, the architect, was careful in his design, knowing that some supernaturals, including fae, are allergic to iron. He used a different metal that gives the same look and feel as wrought iron, but isn't made of the same substance.

A small circular table with a large white flower arrangement greets me as I turn to the right and see my grandmother chatting with the interior designer for Weston Design, Graysin Ravenal. They're staring at the elegant staircase leading to the second floor.

Graysin is pretty in a girl-next-door kind of way. I don't know much about her other than she was in town for a short period of time, then she abruptly left before returning.

"Who is Barbara?" Graysin asks.

"The mayor," my grandmother replies.

"Right."

I approach quietly, so as not to interrupt, but both of them shift their gazes to me.

"Julianna, what are you doing here?" my grandmother asks. "Graysin, this is my granddaughter, Julianna Fairchild. Jules is staying with me while she finishes out her senior year at Havenwood Falls High School."

"It's nice to meet you," Graysin smiles at me.

"You too," I reply and bite my bottom lip, nervous at what I am about to do, as I reach into my bag. "I'm heading over to Founders Day, but wanted to donate this to the library."

With a final resolve, I hand my grandmother the leather-bound copy of *Romeo and Juliet*.

Since Sedona won't take it back and Rowan is acting like a jerk, donating it to the new library feels like my best option at the moment.

My grandmother frowns at it. "That is quite a donation, Jules."

"Rowan . . ." I begin, and then my eyes widen as I catch myself before I continue explaining how I came to own the book. "It was a gift," I quickly recover.

"One which you can't accept." Her voice is firm.

"That is why I'm donating it, Gran," I sigh.

"Smart decision."

"Thank you, Julianna," Graysin interjects.

"No problem," I mumble, and turn to leave.

Just as I'm halfway out the door, I hear my grandmother say, "Those Bishop boys are nothing but trouble."

Rolling my eyes, I take a few steps before bumping into a very hard chest.

Two strong arms reach out to steady me before I tumble down the stairs and off the porch. In an attempt to catch myself, my hands fly out and grab onto the leather bands circling the wrists of the extremely good-looking guy standing in front of me. My gaze glides over the Celtic tattoo on his forearm and slides upward, meeting his sparkly green eyes.

Holy fairies, Everett Weston is hot.

With a chuckle, Everett runs a hand through his dark hair, which is shorter on the sides and curly and messy on top. I take in a deep breath before saying something silly.

"Hey, Julianna, you all right?" he asks with a deep voice.

I nod, trying to act normal. "Yeah. Sorry to run into you like that."

"No worries." He squeezes my arm and steps back, looking around. "In a hurry?"

"Kinda." I try to form a coherent thought. "I was just donating a book to the new library."

Everett offers me a kind smile. "Which one?"

"*Romeo and Juliet.*"

"Ah, William Shakespeare. A classic."

"It is. Anyway, I gave it to Graysin. She's inside."

Sadness and hurt cross his features before he shakes it off and his eyes land on the doorway behind me. He pauses as if he's almost scared to go inside. "Well. I'd better head in. I don't want to be on the receiving end of your grandmother's wrath for missing the ribbon-cutting ceremony."

"No." I smile up at him. "No one wants that."

He winks and steps around me. "See you around, kiddo."

Once he's gone, I release a long breath. Everett Weston has only been in town a few months, but he's stolen the hearts of a lot of the single ladies in Havenwood Falls. I think we all have big crushes on him. If I were older, and he weren't in love with Graysin, he'd be all I see.

The rumbling sound of a motorcycle approaching has me looking to my right and slowly taking the last two stairs. Just as my foot hits the last step, Rowan pulls up.

He stops directly in front of me, idling his bike. "Need a ride?"

Clearing my throat, I shake my head. "Where's your helmet?"

"Concerned about my safety?"

"Brain splatter is hard to scrape off the roads," I counter. "It's also against the law."

Rowan calmly smiles in response, like he doesn't give a rat's ass about the law.

"Where's Taylor?" There is an unstoppable sneer in my voice when I say her name.

"She isn't my girlfriend."

"I didn't ask. Nor do I care," I snip, because I *so* care.

Rowan lifts an eyebrow, the one with the piercing running through it. "She's a family friend."

"I didn't realize the Bishops had family friends," I counter.

His eyes scan me before he scoffs and revs the bike. "You know what? Forget it, flannels. My bike is too dangerous for you anyway. You're better suited with your head buried in a book."

Is he kidding me? "Are you always such a jerk?"

"Are you always this prissy?"

My hands ball into fists. I've never been angry enough to hit someone before, until now. Normally, I'm easygoing and relaxed. It's as if Rowan's crappy personality is rubbing off on me.

"If I am so *prissy*, why do you keep seeking me out?" I question fiercely.

Pressing his lips together, he considers my argument. "Point made."

After a few moments of silence, he stares at me through his long lashes. "Let's go for a ride."

My eyes look back toward the library to make sure my grandmother isn't watching us, before landing on him again. "I can't. I have the pageant crowning later . . ." I trail off.

"I'll have you back in time. Let me take you somewhere."

"So you can kill me and dispose of the body?"

"So we can become better acquainted."

I narrow my gaze. "You want to be friends?"

Blue eyes pierce mine. "Honestly, I have no idea what I want."

The sincerity in his voice strikes a chord with me, and suddenly, I can't remember why I was upset or guarded with him. Like, ever. I stare at him for a moment, knowing I should say no.

It's a simple word. Two letters.

"Do you have a helmet for me?"

"Nope." He flashes a bright grin before he sees I'm not smiling back. His expression turns serious as his eyes bore into me. "I will keep you safe. I swear."

And like a bad horror movie, where the girl doesn't listen to the audience screaming at her not to go into the dark haunted house, his sincere vow causes me to ignore my need for safety. Something inside me knows he will keep me safe, no matter what.

I stare at him for a long moment, continuing to ignore the warning bells going off in my head that Rowan Bishop is nothing but trouble. But they don't seem as loud and aggressive as they have been. His gaze drops to my lips, and the air feels heavy between us. Unbearable even.

"Come on, flannels. Live a little," he encourages, voice low.

I glance once more at the library.

"Fine," I bite out, with a breathlessness that shouldn't be there.

In two steps, I'm by his side. Holding my eyes, Rowan lifts his hand to help me on. After staring at it for the briefest of moments, I slide my palm into his warm, waiting one. Slowly, his fingers wrap around mine, and my heart lurches in my chest at the contact. His touch is doing strange things to my insides. I feel like I'm pulsing with energy —magic even.

I lean closer. He should scare me. I shouldn't be going anywhere with Rowan Bishop, but between the way he's staring at me and the secure way his hand is holding mine, at the moment I feel completely safe. Odd, since he's such an ass. I straddle the back of his bike. Once I'm on, I slide closer to his back and press up against his hard body.

The back of his free hand brushes against my thigh, and I tense. Rowan's palm pushes firmly against my hip, encouraging me forward. I lean toward him until my chest is pressed completely against his back. Squeezing my eyes closed, I pray he can't feel my heart pounding.

He pulls my hand, the one he's holding, around his waist, taking my other hand and moving it around his other side. With a quick motion, he interlocks my fingers so I am wrapped around his body.

Rowan looks over his shoulder, his eyes locking on to mine. "Don't let go."

I nod, unable to speak over the rush of the engine vibrating around my legs.

"I mean it, Jules. If you're going to ride with me, you can't ever let go."

Our eyes stay locked, and I swear the blue depths of his swirl with some sort of magical hypnotic powers, because all I can say in response to the double meaning of his words is, "I won't."

CHAPTER 5

a short time later, Rowan's bike is climbing up Mt. Alexa toward the top of the waterfalls that Havenwood Falls was named for. Once we've reached the halfway point, Rowan turns to the left and takes us off-road, through the dense forest. After a bit, the wooded landscape surrounding us opens up, turning into a secluded, sunshine-filled field of wildflowers.

As I take in the beauty, I realize the small field is filled with my favorite plant and flower, bellflowers. My lips part as I look at the lavender-colored, woodland flowers. Normally they are at their peak in the summer, but what I love about them is they can bloom through October.

Rowan shuts off the bike, but doesn't move. His stiff body alerts me to the fact I am still completely wrapped around him. Quickly, I release his waist and push myself back on the seat, putting a sliver of space between us. After a second, he slides off and turns, getting back on so he's once again straddling it, but is now facing me. After scooting back, he gently picks my legs up, placing each one over his, giving us more room, since the seat is small. I try not to startle at his touch.

When he notices me staring, he tosses me a half smile.

The smirk causes my stare to drop to his mouth. I wonder if he knows how to kiss. I bet he does. Perfect kisses. The kind that make you forget your name and steal your breath. *Holy faeries.* I need to stop looking at him. And thinking about kissing him. Or him kissing me. Or us kissing.

Rowan leans forward, catching my eyes.

He's so close that his lips are almost touching mine. More kissing thoughts ensue.

I suck in a sharp breath, wanting to back away, but I don't.

His lips curve slightly as he picks up a loose section of hair that escaped my braid during the drive up here, twirling it around his finger. "What color is this?"

I frown, because one would think it's obvious. "Lavender."

"Is it naturally this color, or is this part of your human glamour?"

The fae use glamour to hide our pointed ears and other species-telling characteristics.

"Natural." I snatch my hair back. "Since birth."

"And your violet eyes?" he whispers.

A hot flush of shyness sweeps through me. "They're fae in color."

"I like both. The purple colors suit you."

A small smile forms on my lips. "Thanks."

Rowan dips his chin. "My pleasure."

He pushes up his sleeve, revealing a sexy double infinity tattoo on his forearm.

My lips part in shock, because I have the exact same tattoo on my wrist.

I grab his arm, pulling it closer to inspect it. "Is that—"

"The tattoo the Court gave me? Yeah."

At his admission, my own tattoo tingles. I've had it since I was little, a requirement for all permanent supernatural residents of Havenwood Falls. It's so the Court of the Sun and the Moon can keep track of the supernaturals who are supposed to be here. For fae residents, it also lessens our susceptibility to iron, to which we are allergic.

Each being is allowed to pick their design. To be honest, I have no idea why I'd chosen the double infinity symbol. I just figured when I was younger it appealed to me. But to see the same exact tattoo on Rowan is jarring. What are the odds a fae and mage, from two different families—feuding at that—would choose the same symbol? Rare to almost impossible.

As if realizing my recognition of the symbol, his lips thin as he pulls his arm away and covers it back up with the sleeve of his shirt. "It's not a big deal. We all have a tattoo, flannels."

I push up my own sleeve and raise my arm, showing him the tattoo on my wrist.

His eyes widen before he casts a dark look in my direction. "So?"

"So, they match. Our tattoos are mirror images of one another. The same design. Out of all the supernatural friends and family I have, none of us has the exact same design. You do."

His lips curl as he looks me up and down. "Is that your way of confessing your love to me?"

"No, Rowan," I bite out, aggravated, and quickly cover up my tattoo.

"So, what? We happened to pick the same design. It's not a big deal, Jules."

The air between us becomes heavy with tension, because it is a big deal. Why he's ignoring it, I have no idea. It doesn't make any sense. I don't even really know him.

"Whatever," I snap.

Rowan studies me and sighs. "You don't like me or want to hang out with me. Do you?"

"I'm here, aren't I?"

He contemplates my answer. "It's clear you don't like me. So why are you here?"

I stare into the depths of his gaze. His energy seems to hum around me. It's the weirdest feeling, and yet, at the same time, it's familiar, and I just want to sink into and absorb it.

I shrug. "I have no idea why. There's something about you tha—"

"That what?" he prompts.

My lips part to tell him that there is something about him that feels safe and familiar, but for some reason I don't. He'd just throw it back in my face with a snarky comment.

"Nothing. Do you come up here a lot? I mean," I fidget. "You seem to know your way around the mountains. I've lived in Havenwood Falls my entire life, and I didn't know this place existed."

He cocks a smug eyebrow. "It's not a well-known area. Most locals don't know about it."

I tilt my head and bristle when I see him watching me. "Why do you do that?"

"Do what?"

"Look at me like you know me?"

He glances over his shoulder, his lashes hiding his eyes. "I didn't realize I was doing it."

"Rowan." I say his name quietly, gaining his attention.

I want to question him further, to see if he does know me. If I feel familiar, too. But why put the effort into it? He obviously isn't going to give me a straight or honest answer if I push him.

Silence.

Giving up, I pull my gaze from his and look around. "This place is beautiful."

"It is. I like to come up here and breathe."

"Can you not breathe in town?"

"No." His answer is quick and firm.

"Havenwood Falls is not that bad. Small, yes. But . . . there is some charm and beauty to it."

Rowan watches me for a few moments, curious. "The beings in this town are liars. Cheaters. They deceive for game. This town is darker than most know. And uglier than most can see."

"And yet, you got kicked out of eight private schools to come back," I remind him.

"Not for them. Or the town."

"Then what is so important to you here that made you want to come back?"

He watches me with an intense, piercing gaze as he drifts closer. "This very place we are in now. The ghosts that live here and the memories of them that haunt my every moment."

I resist the urge to ask who the ghosts are he speaks of and take a deep breath because I can tell by the way his body is guarded and how he speaks of this place that it is special to him. Sacred even. For some reason, deep within my soul, I know asking him will only bring him more sadness.

"Thank you for bringing me here."

"Sure." He feigns indifference, but I can see the small smile on his lips.

And that one brief moment, where I made him happy and almost smile, it becomes addicting. I want—no, *need*—to keep doing that to him. I need to see his smile and happiness, like I need air.

"Purple. Tacos. A lantern my grandfather gave me. Reading. My family."

Rowan eyes me, confused. "What?"

"My favorite color. My favorite food. Something I can't live without. My favorite pastime. And something I love more than anything," I reply. "Your turn."

I wait, holding my breath, hoping he'll answer and my efforts to get to know him better pan out.

After a stretch of silence, he speaks quietly. "Black, although purple is close. Tacos. My trust fund. The Order. Someone I once knew, who apparently no longer exists . . ." His voice trails off.

At first, I don't respond, ignoring the way my stomach dipped when he mentioned my eye and hair color, absorbing his answers. "You keep mentioning the Order. What is it?"

"My favorite pastime," he replies.

Of course. King of vague. I frown. Another long moment passes between us.

"We have one thing in common." I smile at him. "Tacos."

"Tacos," he repeats, sounding baffled.

Silence falls between us again as I take in nature. A creek divides the grassy, wildflower-filled area and expands into a pond near the falls. The water ripples gently over the rocks. The soft sound is lulling. Large patches of flat, grassy land filled with wildflowers dancing in the sun surround us. It's peaceful. Suddenly, I'm hit with the desire to never leave this place.

"You know, if someone sees us up here, together, we could get in trouble."

"No one will. Trust me."

Trust and Rowan Bishop don't really go together.

"Why are you so afraid to be seen with me?" His eyes search mine.

"I'm not afraid," I argue. "It's just—"

"Just what?"

I wave my hands around, frustrated. "You know our families' sordid history. And, by now, I am sure you are aware of my grandmother's well-respected standing in the community . . ."

A smug smile is plastered across Rowan's face.

"What?"

"The Fairchilds have always been concerned with their *standing* in the community."

My gaze narrows. "With good cause. My family loves this town. My grandfather is—was," I correct myself quickly, "a well-liked resident in Havenwood Falls with family on the Court of the Sun and the Moon. And a distinguished member of the Seelie Court. An elder. Seelie fae are known for our kindness and likability. Something the Bishops should admire and strive to be like. Specifically, your uncle Drayan and your brothers. Everyone knows what they did to my cousin."

"Emeline's death was an accident. My uncle certainly did not intend for his fiancée to fall through the banister and down a flight of stairs. Ask Roman—he was there."

My eyes narrow. "Emeline's fae wings were bound by dark magic when your uncle struck her and she fell to her death! Her neck was broken, Rowan. One of the few ways to kill a fae."

"That is how your grandfather retells the story, Julianna."

"He would know. He was there that day and witnessed it." I grit my teeth.

Rowan seethes. "My uncle, Drayan, lost his fiancée in a tragic accident. And every day since, your family has done nothing but blame mine for her death. We don't practice black magic. Period. This grudge and feud you hold onto—"

"It was your father Rodavan and the Bishops who swore a blood feud over it," I argue.

"Don't be naïve, Julianna. So did Akeel and the Fairchilds."

I start to respond, prepared to throw something else back at him, but stop, realizing this argument is stupid. This . . . this is exactly why our families are fighting years later.

My blood is pumping way too fast in my body for me to calm down. The topic has caused a strange edginess to flow in my veins as we stare at one another. For a brief moment, neither one of us speaks. Rowan's chest rises and falls, and the deep navy in his eyes has turned even darker as we try not to foam at the mouth at one another.

"What happened back then, it has nothing to do with us now." I drop it.

"Agreed. Our families have a long and frankly insane history, Jules." I shiver at my nickname falling from his lips, and that weird familiar feeling brushes over me again. "Let's just leave it in the past and between them. I don't have time to deal with family drama. Or either of my brothers."

"Either of your brothers? What do you mean?"

His jaw flexes. "Ronan is back. I saw him at Founders Day earlier."

At the mention of the middle Bishop brother, I flinch. Ronan Bishop is well known around town as being a ladies' man and troublemaker. He likes to come and go in and out of town, whenever he fancies it. It's been rumored that he's chosen to become a pirate, or something odd.

"Are you not close to either of your brothers?"

"Roman is extremely busy with his company, the Court, and the town. Ever since his wife Jenni died, he's thrown himself into business. And Ronan, when he's in town, follows Callie around like a lost puppy dog. So no, I'm not close to either of my brothers," he replies blandly.

My gaze slips around him to the creek. "I know the feeling. Both my parents were called away on Seelie Court business after my grandfather died. My grandmother works all the time. I think she does it to fill the emptiness my grandfather left after his death. But to be honest, I just feel . . . lonely."

A comfortable and understanding silence falls between us for a short time as we both start to calm down. To be frank, given Rowan is a powerful mage, I'm surprised his magic didn't go off like fireworks, which means he lied earlier. He has excellent control over his abilities.

What is he hiding? Why did he really get sent away?

Rowan clears his throat, his voice thick. "I think it's time we head back."

I nod, disappointed. Why? I have no idea, but for some reason, the thought of leaving him makes me feel icky and sad. As strange and illogical as it is, since he's an ass . . . there is just something about him that calls to me. I hate to admit it, but deep down, I think I like Rowan.

We don't speak as Rowan stands, sits back down and starts the motorcycle.

And as we head back to town, we are silent. Neither of us has anything more to say, lost in our own thoughts and feelings. Once we get down the mountain, Rowan pulls up to the edge of the town center and idles the bike.

Without looking back at me, he waits for me to slide off, which I do, ungracefully. As I stand next to him, my legs feel tight and wobbly from being on his bike. Oddly, now that we've spent more time getting to know one another, it feels like there are miles between us.

"Jules, I—"

"There you guys are." River runs over to us. "Rowan, we're wanted in the Tomb."

"The tomb?" I repeat, my gaze sliding between the two of them.

River and Rowan exchange odd glances before Rowan nods. "Meet you there."

"Yeah. No problem," River replies casually and walks in the direction of the private school, which is odd since it's Founders Day and neither of us has school.

"Secret mission?" I tease.

"Something like that." He smiles. "Thanks for riding with me this morning."

"Thank *you* . . . for the ride," I reply and then cringe at the unintended double meaning.

A deep laugh falls out of him as he winks. "Anytime. See you around, flannels."

I watch as he takes off, and my stomach knots with something unknown. The deep rumble of his motorcycle matches the sexy sound of his laughter. I don't know what it is about him.

What I do know is that Rowan Bishop is the type of boy that breaks hearts, leaving a trail of carnage in his wake. He's trouble. The kind of trouble I don't need. I have a plan, and Rowan isn't part of it.

I STARE outside the window of my AP English Lit class, watching as the snowflakes fall from the gray sky. The elegant white dots dance and swirl in the frigid November air. It's been weeks since Rowan and I last saw one another. Even with school, the drama last month at the homecoming dance, and my night classes at Sun and Moon Academy, Rowan's absence has gifted me endless amounts of time to think about nothing else but him. Trust me, I hate myself for it.

"Miss Fairchild?" Mr. Zander prompts from the front of the class.

I snap my attention to him. "Could you repeat the question?"

The teacher waves a piece of paper at me. "I said, the office would like to see you, Julianna."

Murmuring from my classmates ensues, floating around me—probably because I have never been called to the office. I've never been in any sort of trouble whatsoever, for that matter. I frown, wondering what I could have possibly done. Grabbing my bag, I shove my stuff into it before sliding out of my seat, taking the note from Mr. Zander and making my way to the door.

Just as I step into the empty hallway, the heavy door slams behind me. The loud bang echoes, causing me to jump and my heartrate to pick up. Annoyed at myself for not closing it slowly, I make my way toward the office, but stop just before I get there, when I unexpectedly see Rowan.

He's standing with his hands shoved into the front pockets of his jeans, leaning against the wall. One foot up and one firmly on the floor. He stares at me, his brows slanting low as his lips tip up at one corner, clearly pleased with my presence and approach.

My eyes dart around, but we are the only two in the hallway.

Surprised to see him, I take the last few steps toward him. "What are you doing here?"

"Knitting," he quips, and I roll my eyes.

I cross my arms across my chest and silently wait him out.

He clears his throat. "If I said transferring, would you believe me?"

"No." I'm not sure if he's serious or not. I doubt it, though.

Rowan pushes off the wall so we're standing toe to toe as he looks down at me.

"I don't have time for your games today. I was called to the office, so if you will excuse me," I try to step around him, but he moves quickly and blocks me. "Move, Rowan."

"I sent the note," he whispers.

"What? Why?" I question softly.

"To get you out of class."

"Why?" I repeat.

He half grins. "Because I'm in the mood for tacos."

I crane my neck, meeting his steady gaze. "Are you being serious?"

Rowan's expression becomes solemn. "Let me be clear. I never, ever joke about tacos."

Confused, I look at him. He's serious. "We get an hour for lunch. I can leave campus then."

"It needs to be now." His tone is firm.

I look at my phone. "It's nine in the morning. I can't leave now."

"Why not?"

"I'm in the middle of English Lit."

"No," he argues. "You are in the hallway talking to me, with a note in your hand that excuses you from going back to class."

I arch my brow at him. "Rowan," I sigh. "Don't you have classes today?"

"Come on." He leans in, his lips a sliver from mine. "Live a little, flannels."

"You need to stop calling me that. And you need to stop saying that to me. I do live."

A grin appears on his lips, but it has an edge to it. It's rough and sexy. And suspicious.

"No. You're existing. Buying time until you officially get the hell out of this town."

Damn him for being right. Who is this guy?

My focus slides to the front doors of the school. Am I seriously considering this?

He stares at me for a moment, then jerks his head toward the doors. "What's it going to be?"

I chew on my lip. This is crazy. But holy fairies, he smells good. It's been over a month since I've spent time with him. And for whatever insane reason, I really want to hang out with him.

"Fine, let's do this," I agree, with a great amount of trepidation.

He chuckles and grabs my backpack from me, flinging it over his shoulder, before sliding his hand into mine, and I freeze. I just stand there, staring at our interlocked fingers. And all I can think about is how warm his palm is against mine. For a moment, I forget my name. And how to breathe—as all the muscles in my body tense. With a squeeze of my hand, his eyes find mine.

"You're so damn beautiful," he whispers, and my world stops.

"You're delusional," I barely manage through my dry throat.

"You are—inside and out. Even if you are unaware that you are."

"You've been gone," I accuse. "It's been weeks."

Rowan's eyes bore into me, trying to convey something. "I'm here now."

I nod and ignore the gut feeling I have that there is more meaning behind his answer.

"Come on." He pulls me down a lesser-used hallway and out through a side door.

The minute we step outside, I shiver, having forgotten to grab my coat from my locker.

"Holy crap, it's cold." My teeth chatter.

Rowan looks me over, confused, before he realizes I'm in my thin flannel button-down shirt.

His eyes take in the snow, and quickly, he pulls off his coat, wrapping it around me. The moment his coat covers me, I'm engulfed in warmth, coziness, and his scent.

"Wait, what about you?" I ask. "Won't you freeze?"

"I'm good for a few seconds."

The moment we step off campus, he chants something under his breath. I can't make out the words. An energy swirls around us, bringing with it warmth, and I realize he's spelled us, cocooning us both in a tiny bubble of heat and shielding us from the cold Colorado weather.

"That's convenient," I mutter. "But even away from the school's ward, it's against the rules."

"Keeping you warm is against the rules?"

"Using magic in public," I remind.

He winks, uncaring. "Come on." He pulls me forward. "Tacos!"

CHAPTER 6

We make our way down Main Street until we reach an alley, where the Tacos for Daze food truck is parked to the side. Sky Spill Water owns the restaurant on wheels, and while it's undetermined, it's rumored he's a troll. Sky loves a few things: Jerry Garcia, weed, shouting random Spanish words, and his taco truck. The older Havenwood Falls resident can be seen around town, even in the dead of winter, sporting his gray hair in braids, Hawaiian shirts, weird-patterned yoga pants, and flip-flops. And while his looks and mannerisms are odd—on a good day—his taco truck food is to die for.

Rowan tugs me down the alley, toward the truck. I throw a questioning glance at him.

"Sky parks the taco truck here during off hours," he explains.

A second later, we're standing at the back of the truck where the doors are and with a quick spell, the lock pops open. Looking over his shoulder at me, Rowan wiggles his brows before opening the doors and quickly ushering us in, closing and locking them behind us.

I take in the darkened, empty kitchen area before swinging my attention to Rowan and removing my hand from his. "You pulled me out of class to break into Tacos for Daze and then what? Go for a joy ride? This is so stupid. Sky will be here soon to open."

His lips twitch at that. "Well, I wasn't thinking we'd *steal* the truck, but if you want—"

"NO!" I give him a light push on the arm. "I don't want to steal it.

49

We shouldn't even be in here. It's not open for service. We're totally breaking the law."

"Lawbreaking is all part of the fun!"

"I am pretty sure my parents will disagree when they find out I did this."

"Key word is *if.* Now, what's your favorite menu item?"

I cock my head and narrow my eyes. "The Mexicali Blues Tacos."

Rowan laughs. "Me, too."

"Oh, and the Good Lovin' Nachos are amazing."

"I also like the Ramble on Rose Taquitos."

I nod my agreement, because those taquitos are addictive.

"Is it weird that Sky names food after Grateful Dead songs?" I ask, relaxing a bit.

"Since I've seen him hanging out with Adrian Roca at the pot dispensary, no."

My eyes widen. "There's a pot dispensary in town? And why are you hanging out there?"

That weird look crosses his features, the one he gets when he can't decide if I'm being serious or not.

"You really are sheltered," he responds faintly.

I bristle, because for some absurd reason, his statement annoys the crap out of me. "If by *sheltered* you mean I've lived in the same town all my life. Have a perfect GPA. Enjoy charitable work. Love reading. And don't break the law—well, normally. Then, yes. I guess I'm sheltered."

"All I meant is that you hang out at the country club with high society. You have no idea what goes on in this town. It's not all charm. No matter how many tulips they plant in the square."

"It's November. It's too cold for tulips." I cinch my forehead.

Rowan laughs at my expression. "What's wrong?"

"I guess I'm a little boring," I mutter under my breath. "And sheltered."

"I never said you were boring." His arms spread out wide. "On the contrary. You skipped school with me, flannels, and broke into the town taco truck. That is nothing if not exciting."

I roll my eyes at him.

"I'm starving. So, what will it be today? Your normal tacos or something different?"

My gaze meets his. What is it about Rowan Bishop that ignites something in me? It's like he makes me feel alive. He was right about one thing earlier: I have been going through the motions for a long time. Always feeling like there is something missing. Being around him, as cliché as it sounds, makes me feel complete. Less like I am simply buying time until I go to college.

I'm always smiling and being cordial at all the country club events. Being polite to elders and respectful to everyone around me. Not a doormat, just agreeable. And today, I'm done.

Rowan makes me want to—just have fun!

"Are you cooking? Because I have no clue how to use any of this equipment."

"Magic is," he replies, and with a flick of his wrists, the truck's power comes to life.

"O-kay." I throw him an amused look.

"What's it going to be, Jules? Your usual? Or something new?" he asks again curiously.

Lifting my chin, I smile. "I am going to epically regret this, but I'll have a Hell in a Bucket."

Rowan's brows rise. "I never would have taken you for a spicy girl."

I shrug and tease, "It's not like you know everything about me."

Rowan's lips purse, and he falls quiet for a moment before speaking again. "I guess not."

I peer at him, trying to gauge his sudden sullen expression.

The burners suddenly come to life around us, and without another word, I watch as Rowan makes his way around the small kitchen space, cooking. It turns out Rowan Bishop is an amazing chef, and with a little magic, he delivers a kickass, scorching taco. One that was totally worth missing classes for. After scarfing down the first two, I have him make me two more.

Stuffed, I rub my stomach while we're sitting on the unusually clean floor of Sky's truck.

"We need to clean this mess up or Sky's going to kill us," I moan, looking around.

"I cooked," he states. "You clean."

"What makes you think I can clean all this?" I wave my hand around.

He laughs at my response. "You're Seelie fae. Don't you have gifts?"

"I'm not Tinker Bell," I counter. "I don't carry fairy dust and fly. Besides," I huff. "My fae gifts center around truth and deceit. Not cleaning." I give him a pointed glare. "Think of me as more of a lie detector rather than a cleaning crew."

"Noted. No lying to you," he mumbles and stands, holding out his hands to me.

I slide mine into his, and he tugs me up and toward him. The force causes me to wobble off balance, and I have to place my hands on his chest to stop from falling into him. Rowan steadies me by curling his fingers around my hips, and I draw in a shallow breath at the contact, taken aback at the energy jumping between us. I don't move as Rowan stares down into my eyes.

Every inch of my body is hyperaware of his, even the breaths moving between his lips.

My attempt at trying to focus on something other than the way his hands curve perfectly around me is an epic fail, because all I can focus on is the warmth of his palms as they hold me.

"You have a piece of cilantro on your lip." His voice is shaky as he lifts his hand, and with his thumb, he brushes off the tiny green leaf.

A crooked smile appears on him when I shiver at his touch.

I wish I had enough experience in situations like this to come up with something clever and flirty to say, but all I can do is stare into his intense gaze and barely whisper, "Thank you."

Confusion crosses his expression as he leans forward, his lips parting slightly. Rowan's thumb traces my hip, brushing over it, back and forth. We stay like this, caught up in the moment. My heart stutters as anticipation builds while he searches my eyes. Every second passes slowly.

As he lowers his head toward mine, my breath catches in my throat.

When his breath caresses my lips, I freeze altogether.

I'm torn between desperately wanting to meet him halfway, and to pull back. Away from him.

Rowan's expression strains as if he's waging his own internal battle.

The lock on the back doors suddenly rattles, and dread pushes through me as the two doors fly open. I take in a sharp breath when Rowan jerks back away from me. In one fluid movement, he puts a healthy distance between us, leaving me feeling surprised and disappointed.

"Hey, man. What are you two doin' in here?" a slurred, Hispanic-accented voice questions.

Sky Spill Water.

Heat radiates off my cheeks when I meet Sky's droopy gaze.

"Julianna? *You're* stealin' my truck?" he asks, surprised to see me. "This is unexpected."

And awkward. Super awkward. I don't even want to think about what would have happened if he hadn't showed up and interrupted us. My cheeks burn even more at the thought.

"Sorry, we were jus—"

"Leaving," Rowan grins at Sky in his easy, carefree manner, stepping in front of me and placing me behind him, almost as if he is protecting me. With his right hand, Rowan drops a wad of cash down on the counter. "That should cover everything. Sorry about the inconvenience."

And then some, I think to myself, taking in all the hundred dollar bills rolled up.

Sky's face scrunches. "Ah, man. I wish I had known it was you, Julianna, when Eloise Sinclair said someone was breaking into my taco truck." He looks guilty.

"I'm so sorry we broke in," I reply, sincerely. "It's fine, though, we'll just go."

"No, girlie, it's not. Had I known, I wouldn't have brought the sheriff in on this."

"The sheriff?" Rowan repeats, just as Sheriff Kasun appears.

"Oh, and this dude, too." Sky throws a thumb over his shoulder at Elsmed Fairchild.

"It's all right, Sky, I was with Sheriff Kasun when he received the call," Elsmed states, looking at me. "Julianna is family. It's good I'm here."

I try not to bristle under the fae elder's heavy, stern stare. Elsmed Fairchild is on the Court of the Sun and the Moon. He's known for his intimidating piercing blue glares and serious demeanor. I put up my mind's shield, knowing he has telepathic abilities and can read thoughts.

Sensing my block, he throws a withering glare my way. At times, Elsmed reminds me of my grandfather. My grandfather was less cold and formal. Not as intimidating as his cousin is.

"Oh, okay," Sky slurs like he's heavily medicated.

"Julianna. Rowan." Sheriff Kasun's voice is firm. "You'll both have to come with me."

I swallow through my now-dry throat. My face flushes for the third time in ten minutes.

For the love of fairies, could this moment get any worse? Oh, wait, yes it can.

"Do I smell magic in the air?" The sheriff stares at Rowan.

"Among other things." Elsmed's focus shifts to Sky, who places his palms up in a surrendering motion, while giving the fae elder an *I have no idea what you are talking about* look.

"What can I say?" Rowan's relaxed tone matches his stance as he throws his arm around my shoulder and pulls me closer to him. "Young, forbidden love is magical," he taunts.

"That isn't what I meant," Sheriff Kasun replies.

"Take your Bishop hands off Fairchild blood," Elsmed growls out.

I try to step out of Rowan's protective hold, but he doesn't let me. "Watch it, old man."

"This isn't what it looks like," I squeak out, my lame attempt at an interruption to prevent Rowan from further threatening a member of the Court, which will not end well for him. Especially because this one is family.

Fairchild family.

"What it looks like, Julianna, is that my cousin's granddaughter is about to commit grand theft auto. In addition, you're perpetrating truancy by not being in school. Shall I go on? Let's not ignore the breaking and entering charge. I have yet to point out that you are consorting with a Bishop." The fae lowers his voice. "A Luna Coven member, who used magic in public."

"We didn't mean—" I begin, but he cuts me off.

"Come on, kids." Sheriff Kasun motions for us to join them outside of the truck.

My heart sinks, because both Sheriff Kasun and Elsmed are enforcers of the Court's rules that apply to supernatural beings, which means there is no talking our way out of this. They have no choice but to turn us in to the Court for using magic in public.

"This will upset your grandmother," Elsmed sighs angrily. "I can only hope that this . . . Bishop somehow spelled you. A powerful spell that made you lose all sense of right and wrong."

"Spells are badass." Sky sways as if he's about to pass out.

With an annoyed sigh, Elsmed waves his hand in front of Sky.

Sky blinks rapidly and frowns, scratching his head.

My guess is he used fae magic to make Sky forget what he heard about spells. Ironic.

"That is enough, Elsmed," another deep voice floats into the truck, and I hear Rowan curse.

Roman Bishop.

Unable to breathe past the ball of fear choking me, I swallow and squeeze my eyes closed. If Roman is standing outside with Sheriff Kasun, Elsmed, and Sky, this is about to get so much worse. I keep my eyes closed, praying this is all just a bad dream.

One where I wake up and instead of the Bishops and Fairchilds feuding, once again, this time in the back of a taco food truck, Rowan and I are surrounded by bellflowers, running carefree like children in a sun-filled field.

OVER THE PAST FEW DAYS, things have officially gone from bad to worse. After being arrested and released into the custody of our families, Rowan and I were given a date and time to appear before the Court of the Sun and the Moon. Since we are being charged with using magic in public, if found guilty, the Court of the Sun and the Moon will decide our punishment instead of the town's public judicial system.

Today, Rowan and I are in the secret offices of the Court in the back of City Hall for our formal proceeding. The large room has a dais up front for Court members to sit and preside over the trials and sentencing of supernaturals who have broken magical laws.

Elsmed, Gran, and I are sitting across from the dais on one side of the aisle.

Roman and Rowan are on the other.

My heart grows heavy, knowing how much trouble we're in.

As we wait for the Court members, I take in the Bishop brothers. While both are tall, tanned, and muscular, that is where the similarities end. Roman has slick black hair, bright ocean-blue eyes, and a small scar under his left eye. It's barely noticeable unless you are close to him, like I am now. He is also formally dressed in tailored pants, a silk shirt, and expensive leather shoes.

Unlike Rowan's casual jeans and motorcycle style.

"Allow me to speak," Roman tells his brother quietly. "The Court may bring up how you are only a few weeks into your academic year and are already in jeopardy of failing due to your lack of interest in class attendance and participation."

My grandmother sighs beside me while mumbling under her breath. Given she despises muttering, it's an odd thing to hear her do. "Breaking and entering, Julianna. Skipping school," her voice becomes more stern and loud. "I would expect this from a Bishop." Gran snaps her hand at Rowan. "But not you," she scolds.

I cringe at the tone in her voice, meeting my grandmother's steely gaze.

"It's not totally Rowan's fault." I sigh, and she levels me with a glare.

"Watch how you speak of and to my brother, Mrs. Fairchild." Roman's voice is cool as he stares at Gran, less than amused.

"Your *brother* is a criminal. And needs to stay away from my granddaughter," she snaps back.

"While I agree with you that there is no need for the two to be around each other, I will not allow you to insult him," Roman fires back. "So, again, use your words carefully, human."

At the reminder that my grandmother is human, the room falls silent, to an almost ear-piercing level. Miss Mary Beth is one of a handful of humans who know about the supernatural residents in Havenwood Falls and the Court. That said, she is still not immune to magic.

"Easy, Roman," Elsmed advises.

"Gran, stop." My voice is soft. I don't know if she heard me, so I repeat her name.

Finally, she breaks out of the Roman Bishop staredown trance captivating her.

My grandmother lifts her chin, unintimidated by Roman as the Court members enter and take their seats in front of us on the dais. Presiding over our proceedings today are Mayor Barbie Stuart, Lilith Blackstone, Michaela Petran, and Lawrence Mills.

"Thank you all for being here today," Mayor Barbie starts. "Due to family ties that are considered conflicts of interests, Roman and Elsmed, you both are recused from today's vote. However, each of you may speak on behalf of Julianna and Rowan if they or you wish."

"Sheriff Kasun isn't here," Gran points out. "This is more of a legal matter for Julianna."

"Sheriff Kasun is indisposed at the moment," Barbie replies.

"Sky isn't pressing legal charges, Miss Mary Beth," Michaela points out. "Rowan took care of any damages that were done with a monetary payment."

My grandmother gives her a short, curt nod. "Then we're done here."

Lawrence's voice booms in the room. "There is the matter of magic being used in public."

"Elsmed's or mine?" Rowan fires back in challenge, and I press my lips together.

"Watch it," Elsmed warns.

"Jules didn't use her fae powers," Rowan interjects. "Therefore, she didn't break any rules."

"She may not have used her powers, but it is alleged that you did, Rowan. Julianna was with you at the time, and therefore, is guilty by association," Lilith informs.

Rowan and I fall quiet. This meeting seems to have little to do with our input anyway. They have already made up their minds about us and what we are and aren't guilty of.

"I can't fathom how you've come to the conclusion my granddaughter is guilty by association, or had anything to do with Rowan choosing to use his mage gifts," Gran argues.

"What proof do you have that my brother used his gifts?" Roman asks. "Do you have any proof? I mean, other than Ric and Elsmed's theories about smelling magic in the air?"

"He is a Bishop. That is all the proof you need," my grandmother snips.

"I will not warn you again to show my brother respect, Mrs. Fairchild," Roman snarls.

"Stop," I yell before I can stop myself. "Rowan did nothing wrong. I was cold, and he simply created a heat bubble so I wouldn't freeze to death. In the truck, he ignited some flames and turned on the lights so we could cook a few tacos. He didn't use magic on humans or hurt anyone."

My grandmother gives me a look that that makes my mouth close with a quick snap.

A disappointed look comes at me from Michaela—like I had just proven Gran's *Bishops are evil* theory—and a sinking feeling settles in my stomach that I have just been baited into a confession.

"I know I'm new, but no harm was done to humans. Sky isn't upset.

In fact, I bet he's using Rowan's money to buy more pot this very minute," Michaela points out. "But—"

"Regardless," Barbie interrupts, cutting her off. "The facts are you both skipped school. You both broke into the truck. And while only one of you may have used magic, you did it together."

"I take full responsibility," Rowan speaks up. "Julianna is an innocent bystander. I talked her into everything. Let her go, punish me and ban me from town, and let's be done with the insanity."

Roman's eyes flick to his brother. "Sun and Moon is your last chance to graduate. There is no banishing you from town," he growls out. "I will not allow it."

"Last chance to graduate?" Michaela repeats. "I have an idea."

Barbie nods her approval for Michaela to go on. Since I don't know Michaela, my stomach twists, wondering where she is going with this idea she seems to have suddenly had.

"Julianna can tutor Rowan. Make sure he is meeting his class requirements and graduates."

"No," Roman, Elsmed, and my grandmother all shout at the same time.

"Circumstances and common sense make this seem pretty cut and dry to me," Michaela continues. "Julianna isn't at fault, but she was there, so she needs to be held accountable. Given that she just won Miss Teen Havenwood Falls, I am going to assume that she has a high GPA and is actively involved in community service. Therefore, community service in the form of tutoring Rowan isn't a stretch as punishment for her poor choices. As for Rowan, it's my opinion that he has been punished enough."

Michaela looks around, meeting the eyes of everyone in the room, landing her focus on Rowan, who dips his chin. The rest of the Court members fall silent.

I frown, not understanding what she means.

"If the Court agrees, Rowan, your punishment comes down to this: you show up for every tutoring session. Every. Single. One. You pass all of your classes, and you graduate on time. If you fail to accomplish this, we will see both you *and* Julianna in here again, at which time the Court won't be so lenient."

My grandmother's eyes widen. "Michaela, I like you very much, but that is absurd. Julianna is an upstanding member of this community.

She has never been in trouble. You are placing her entire future in jeopardy. To help a Bishop who is about to be kicked out of school and is a menace to this town," she huffs. "Bishops and Fairchilds do not consort."

"Miss Mary Beth, with respect, Julianna placed her own future in jeopardy when she chose to commit these infractions." Michaela lifts her chin. "When I took my seat on this Court I became well aware of the situation between the Bishops and Fairchilds," she replies, cryptically. "I don't agree with what you all have done, or are currently doing, to keep them apart."

"Thank you, Michaela," Barbie interjects. "I happen to agree with your suggestion. Julianna will tutor Rowan two days a week as her community service. At tea the other day, Miss Mary Beth, you mentioned Julianna was taking two evening classes at Sun and Moon Academy. For one hour prior to each of her classes, they can meet in the library on the Academy's campus." She looks at us sternly. "And you must *remain* on campus."

"Lilith, I believe you hold the proxies of those Court members who are not present?" Lawrence inquires.

"I do. My vote today will also count as theirs," Lilith replies.

"Excellent. All in favor of Julianna tutoring Rowan?" Barbie poses.

She, Michaela, and Lilith all vote in favor, with Lawrence disagreeing.

"Majority wins. Our ruling stands," Lilith states.

No one breathes, the air having been ripped from the room by the ruling.

"This is insanity," my grandmother's taut voice shatters the silence.

"The Court has ruled, Miss Mary Beth," Barbie warns.

"You have no idea what you are doing, or what you've done," Roman barks out.

"Oh, I think we do," Michaela challenges from her seat. "This ends, now."

I look over at Rowan, dumfounded because I'm not following the conversation.

He seems to be, though, and couldn't look more pleased. An icy sensation trickles down my spine as I bite my lip to keep myself from vocalizing any more protests or admissions.

"This is not over," my grandmother sulks. "Let's go, Julianna."

She storms to the door with me following as I avoid my

grandmother's gaze, ashamed of the embarrassment and pain I know this is causing her on top of losing my grandfather.

Behind us, more arguing ensues.

Once we are in the hallway, my grandmother turns to me. "They have cursed your fate."

CHAPTER 7

$\mathcal{T}$he Sun and Moon Academy library is absolutely insane. Two stories of books, many bound in leather, are nestled away on dust-free mahogany shelves. Silence engulfs you as you walk through the large open space. Stained glass windows take up an entire wall, letting in the smallest hint of natural light, but the beams are tinted depending on the angle of the sun coming through the colored glass.

The quietness and hand-carved, expensive-looking wood makes this place feel sacred. Religious even. The cathedral domed ceiling, painted with supernatural creatures, feeds right into the sacred feel. Inhaling, I bask in the scent of leather and paper. The smell of books.

I check the time on my cell, noting I'm five minutes early, and look around. A few people are mingling or sitting around the room, but my attention immediately falls to the guy in the back corner. He wears a black hoodie covering his head, and the book in his hands blocks his face from view. Regardless, my skin tingles and the hair on my arm stands on end as my body goes on high alert, knowing it's Rowan.

Tonight is my first night of tutoring him since the Court's bomb-dropping ruling, which, according to my grandmother, is the end of the world. She hasn't spoken to me in two days. I'm also grounded for the rest of my life, per my parents, who were not too pleased to learn of my offenses. Although I swear I saw a small smile on my mother's lips when they video-called to basically yell at me for losing all sense of self-respect and common sense—my dad's words—after my grandmother had already gone up one side of me and down the other.

Strangely intrigued that he's reading, I watch Rowan, or the curse, as he is now known in the House of Fairchild, out of the corner of my eye. He's focused on his book, seemingly oblivious to me. And yet, somehow, I know without a doubt that Rowan is aware of every inch of space and everything that surrounds him, including me.

Something I find both curious and frightening about him.

A sense of déjà vu hits me as I study him. This odd sensation overtakes me that I've seen him reading that same book before. Only for some absurd reason, I picture him under a tree, with the sunlight bouncing off his hair as I lay my head in his lap and he reads out loud.

Shaking my head, I tell myself it is just a fantasy, because daydreams about Rowan Bishop are easy things to imagine and get lost in. Yet, there has always been something that felt familiar about him, which is odd, given I'm certain our paths have never crossed before now.

I'm convinced I would remember meeting him; his mere existence is not something I could easily forget. Who could? I mean, look at him. I tilt my head, still staring. At the same time, a tiny voice in my head and a feeling deep in my soul keeps telling me I'm wrong, that I know him.

He shifts in his seat, and the motion pulls me out of my own thoughts. With careful steps, I approach the table where he sits, my focus on his fingers curled around the book. Once I am next to him, I pull out the chair, sit, and watch him through my lashes. He seems to be making a point of not looking at me, and it's starting to aggravate me . . . more than it should. It's also making me feel flustered, unnerved, and oddly hurt. Especially since he's the one who got us into this.

Quiet hangs in the air between us as I stubbornly wait for him to speak first.

"You came," he mumbles after a long time, and I jump at the sound.

"You're surprised to see me?" I ask in a hushed tone, confused.

Rowan closes his book and leans toward me, invading my personal space. "I figured the Fairchilds would have found a loophole to prevent you from being here with me."

I hold his intense glare. "I'm here. For you. And with you, Rowan."

He sits back in his chair. His eyes burn into me, and a shiver runs through my body. Appearing bored, Rowan shifts his head further back into his hood, making it impossible to see his expression or eyes anymore.

The desire to reach under his hood and lift it back from his face is so overwhelming, I have to ball my hands into fists under the table as I glare at the book.

"I'm sorry for what my grandmother said in the Court. It was wrong, and she shouldn't have insinuated that you had anything to do with my choices simply because of your last name. I chose to go with you that day. We're both at fault equally for the trouble we got in," I whisper.

He doesn't say anything in response. I remain quiet, thinking I've said the wrong thing and hurt him, but when I lift my gaze back to him, he's watching me with an unreadable expression.

"Can I ask you something?" I question in a quiet tone.

A strange feeling comes over me when he doesn't answer me. What is his deal tonight?

"You stole the book you gave me, then paid for it. We broke into the taco truck, but after, you paid for everything. Why? Why pull me out of school with a fake note? Why not just wait until I had my hour off and take me out to lunch, during normal business hours, and save yourself what I'm guessing was a lot of money and trouble? I told you I had permission to leave campus. Why does everything you do have to be an eff-you to the Court and the laws? Does it have something to do with what was said about you by the Court—is it revenge?"

Rowan crosses his arms over his broad chest. His teeth play with his lip piercing while he's quiet before he answers. "You saw how everyone reacted to us being together. The stigma that comes with having Bishop as your last name in this town. You've made it pretty clear you don't want to be seen around town with me for that very reason. Our families, the history . . . it's a nightmare. I get it. But," he pauses, and something deep in my gut stirs as we hold each other's gaze. "You like tacos. I like you. The way I did it, I didn't give you the option of saying no. If I had asked you to lunch, you would have said no. This way, I shielded you from the awkwardness with friends at school and the busybodies in town. My way, no one bothered us."

My brows pull together. "You were protecting me from being seen with you?"

"In a way," he replies.

"That is stupid reasoning."

"Maybe. And," he leans back into my personal space, looking up at me from under his hood.

"And what?"

"And I think you're pretty tightly wound, flannels. You could use a little fun in your life."

"And fun to you is breaking laws and rules?"

His face turns serious. "It's not about the criminal activity."

"Then what is it about?"

"It's about feeling alive and free. Not always being perfect. Or doing what is expected." He slides closer, leaning in so our lips are almost touching. "It's about not allowing others to dictate who you are. Or what you want. As long as no one gets hurt, it's just about free will and control."

At his words, I fall speechless. Rowan's alluring smile and magnetic energy seem to cause my circuits to short out and my brain to stop functioning properly. I can't explain what I feel, but attraction doesn't seem to cover it.

I keep my voice low and level. "I disagree. It seems to me you're the one hurting."

Rowan's hand comes up and gently cups my cheek. I try not to flinch at the unexpected movement, because his touch makes me feel protected and safe. "I want to show you something."

My eyes dart around. "We aren't supposed to leave. I am supposed to be tutoring you."

"We can't leave campus. What I am planning to show you is in this building. On campus. Just as the Court directed," he counters, holding my gaze. "Trust me. It will explain things."

Just as I am about to give in, my phone goes off, pulling my attention to it. Several quick texts come in from Zal, asking how the tutoring is going. She thinks the entire punishment is ridiculous. So, being a good, nosey friend, she's staying on top of things and watching out for me.

I pull my gaze from Rowan and reply to my friend, grateful for the space to breathe and come to my senses, because he makes me all crazy inside. Once I hit send, I look back at him. "We have an hour. Tell me what classes you're taking and need help in, so we can figure out your learning style and the best way to approach our tutoring sessions to make them more efficient."

Rowan gives me a self-assured graceful smirk and leans toward me again. "All right, flannels. Your way tonight." He pulls out his iPad and some textbooks, placing them on the table.

"You need to stop calling me that." I watch him toss his stuff on the table.

"Why?"

"Because. I don't wear flannel pajamas."

"How would I know that?" He flashes me a bright smile. "Or is that your subtle way of inviting me over sometime to confirm what you wear, or don't wear, to bed?"

I press my lips into a hard line. "You're such a jerk. Has anyone ever told you that?"

"Every single day."

I stare at him in disbelief. "I don't even know what to say to you. Let's just study."

"Or," he stands abruptly, startling me, holding out his hand. "You can come with me."

"Rowan," I growl, having thought we were done with this.

"Come on. Ten minutes, tops."

Sighing, I frown at his hand. "Is this illegal?"

"No."

"I don't believe you." Although my fae gifts aren't sensing he's lying.

"Given our history, your disbelief is understandable." He waits as I contemplate.

His scent wraps around me, and I relax, as if my body recognizes him and reminds me that I don't need to fight my desire to take his hand. My heart keeps telling me to go wherever, and whenever, he invites me to go. My head, well, that is a different story. Yeah, I am a hot mess.

Sensing my resolve to say no is crumbling, Rowan lifts a knowing brow at me.

I chew on my lower lip, and with a heaving groan, I give in to my heart. Pushing my chair back, I slide my hand into his. When his fingers interlace with mine this time, my pulse quiets.

Oddly, my entire demeanor calms the moment I touch him.

My eyes settle on his steady gaze. "You have twenty minutes. Then, we're in here studying."

"Scout's honor."

I narrow my eyes at him. "Were you ever a scout?"

"Nope." He pops his *p*. "I was too busy getting arrested."

"Figures," I mumble under my breath.

He grins at me. "Come on."

He leads me out of the library, through a few empty hallways, and then down an old spiral staircase located in a vacant hallway. From the looks of the stonework, the staircase is original.

After what feels like forever, we walk down a dead-end stone hallway. It's lined on both sides with backlit alcoves, each one highlighting marble statues of men and women from their shoulders up to their heads.

"Planning to kill me and bury me here?" I look around at the unfamiliar part of the school.

"After I show you this, it might be the other way around," he replies.

Once we reach the end of the hallway, Rowan steps up to the last statue. The plaque on the sculpture reads *Zeus*. I scrunch my nose because the guy sculpted in the white stone is definitely not the Greek god Zeus. Rowan places his hand on the statue and shakes it a little.

I throw an impish look at him. "You want me to deface school property with you?"

Ignoring me, he lifts his thumb to the eye of the man, and a small teal light scans his thumbprint. Seconds later, a hidden door in the wall behind the sculpture opens without a sound.

Rowan's grip on my hand tightens as he guides me around the column the sculpture is displayed on, leading me into a dark entryway. There are no lights except for a spotlight shining on another doorway in front of us. I stare in awe at the two double-wide wooden doors towering over us from floor to ceiling, carved with intricate patterns.

At the very top sits a metal plaque with script that reads: *In the Tomb of the Order the brave shall live forever.* In the center, spread across both doors, the letters T and O are overlapped in a circle of teal and gold, surrounded by what appear to be astrological signs.

I risk a glance at Rowan. "What is this?"

"This . . . is the gateway to the Tomb."

"The tomb?" I repeat. *Why does that sound familiar?*

Rowan places his right hand in the middle of the O, and after a moment, the gold ring around the teal turns clockwise, and the doors click. With a creak, they open to reveal a long, medieval-looking room. Surprised, I step in front of Rowan and take in the secret chamber. What the heck?

Rowan moves in close behind me and leans over my shoulder. When his chest brushes my back, a burst of heat encompasses me, feeling like heaven. I lean back, longing to soak in more of his warmth, holding back a small gasp at how amazing the energy flowing between us feels.

His breath tickles the outer part of my ear when he speaks. "Welcome to the Tomb of the Order of Castor," he says in a hushed voice and steps around me, tugging me into the space.

I stumble a few steps before having to stop and then look around, taking everything in.

"This was the original library when the school was first built," he explains. "So, technically, we're still in the library, per the Court's orders. I know how fond you are of rules, flannels."

One of my brows arches at his disheveled, bad-boy smirk, and he winks at my response. Shaking my head, I glance around the teal and gold room. Dark, rich wood covers the floor and bottom portion of the walls. Large stones, painted teal, line the windowless walls.

A heavy dark wooden table sits in the middle of the space with seating for at least ten. The chairs and table remind me of knights and kings. Gold velvet drapes frame the walls on the left and right side of the room, and the ceiling has an intricate wooden honeycomb pattern, with the same astrological signs decorating the panels. An old-fashioned metal chandelier hangs from the middle, over the table, softly lit with flickering amber lights.

I try to keep my mouth from falling open in awe as I look around, but it's hard.

"What is all this?" I ask. "The Tomb? The Order of Castor?"

"You wanted answers to why I do what I do. Why I stole the book. Why I push the boundaries of the Court. Of the town's laws." He takes a step forward. "Well, this is why, Jules."

"I don't understand."

"The Order of Castor, otherwise known as 'The Order,' is a secret society here at Sun and Moon Academy. An elite ten. All seniors from both the Academy and Havenwood Falls High. Male and female. Each a supernatural being from prominent Havenwood Falls families. Our rituals and members are kept confidential. New members are inducted every fall during Founders Day." His voice is deep and husky.

"Wait," I interrupt. "Is that why River said you had a meeting in the *Tomb* on Founders Day?" I look around, not waiting for him to answer. "This is the Tomb. Is River a member also?"

Rowan dips his chin. "This chamber is known to members, or Originals, as the Tomb."

"What is it exactly that the Order does?" I ask, my voice full of wariness.

Rowan's piercing eyes draw my attention. I can't make out the expression on his face, but it is intense as he fixes his focus on me. Something about his stare makes me shift uncomfortably.

"We are the future generation of the Court of the Sun and the Moon. Most of us have family sitting on it. So, many of us will take over their seats at some point. In the meantime, consider us a supernatural fraternity. Once a month, we plan something fun to do as a group. Something that pushes the boundaries and rules."

"Like motorcycle racing on the mountain?" I pin him with a glare.

"We like to have fun and live a little, Jules."

"And this room is where you what? Meet and plan your events?"

"That. And we can use our gifts in here without being detected."

"Does the school know?"

"No. Only previous and current members know about the Order."

"How long has this existed?"

"Since 1899, when the first senior class established the Order of Castor."

"How are members chosen?"

"Some are grandfathered in because of their bloodlines. Others are pledged in. To keep identities confidential, each member chooses and is assigned a nickname from literature or myth. We don't use real names in or outside this room, once a member has been initiated."

"What's your nickname?"

He pauses before a playful smile crosses his lips. "Romeo."

I roll my eyes. "That's unexpectedly cliché."

"Seemed fitting. I am handsome and intelligent."

The intensity in his gaze causes my skin to heat. "You're also impulsive and immature. Though, like the character, your idealism and passion make you extremely likable."

He chuckles. "See. You are tutoring me—in English Lit. Still playing by the rules."

I walk around the room, letting my fingers run over the table as I speak. "Romeo wasn't interested in violence, only love. Is that why you picked an idealistic character to represent you?"

"No." He turns away. "Like Romeo, I am a son born into a house known to be sworn enemies of an aristocratic family in the town I live in. A feud that was started over love."

My gaze snaps to his, and I still. A breath escapes me when I realize how similar our story is to that of the classic. Juliet was a naïve girl who fell in love with the son of her family's great enemy, trusting her life and future to him. Refusing to believe the worst about him, even when there was proof of a fight between cousins. Is that me in this scenario?

"When does pledging start?" I change the subject.

He crosses his arms as he looks at me. "Right before school starts."

"Did you pledge, or are you grandfathered in?"

"I'm grandfathered in, but I still had to go through initiation."

"What did that entail?" I ask, feeling like I already know.

"When my name was approved, the Originals decided that as part of my induction, I had to steal the book of the character I picked," he admits. "We do that sometimes. Break rules and crook."

"Crook?"

"Stealing. Small things, keepsakes, heirlooms, or other artifacts . . . stuff."

My mouth falls open. How silly of me to assume any of this was about me.

"I'd hate to see what the person who picked Zeus had to do," I mutter under my breath, before something hits me. "Wait, that's what you were doing in Shelf Indulgence that day?"

"Yeah."

"Why did you give the book to me then?"

He shrugs. "Believe it or not, I do have some morals. I didn't want to flat-out steal it. Knowing who you were, and having heard about your reputation, I assumed you would return it. Being the Good Samaritan you are and all. But then you went and donated it to the library."

"Sorry for ruining your big plans," I tease. "When I tried to return it, she said it was already paid for. That was before I donated it."

"Sedona was well compensated for the trouble."

"Like Sky?" I counter. "Was that an assignment, too?" I accuse, feeling infinitely small.

Something flickers over his face. Anger? Regret? Neither of us look away.

"No, Julianna. That was me wanting to spend time with you because I like you. And tacos."

Keeping quiet, I hold his gaze, unable to shake the nagging feeling that something is going on here, something more than just Rowan liking me.

"Why are you telling me all this? If it's all a secret?" I ask.

"I am trusting you with this because I want you to trust me."

"Why?"

He cocks his head. "Because one day, I'll need you to fall back on your trust in me."

CHAPTER 8

I stare at my half-eaten turkey burger and fries, moving them around on my plate, praying to whatever fae deity is listening that I can fade into the booths of Burger Bar. In the reflection of the metal table, I see Zal, Paisley, and Makenna with their heads together, plotting in hushed voices.

Paisley is totally into this guy, Cole. We've all gone to school with him for years, but this summer, Cole went through his awakening, and now he's getting a lot of female attention. My cousin has become slightly obsessed. He's all she talks about these days. And right now, Zal and Makenna are feeding into her fangirl drooling. Apparently, boy-craziness runs in the family.

I sigh and force myself to think about anything other than Rowan. He and I have had a few more tutoring sessions since he introduced me to the Order and the Tomb. But he hasn't spoken another word about the secret society, or what we discussed that day. Even so, I can't let go of his last words to me in the Tomb—a plea for trust and belief in him.

A high-pitched squeal from across the table has my attention lifting back to my friends.

"What's going on?" I ask.

Paisley nods her head toward the door, where River, Cole, and Rowan have strolled in. My cousin's violet eyes light up with a mixture of excitement and longing as she watches them take a booth in the back with a view of the river. Zal and I catch each other's gazes, and we share the same quiet thought. Paisley's high level of elation at Cole's appearance is a little disturbing.

Zal leans toward me as Paisley and Makenna focus on one another. "You okay?"

I nod, toying with my straw. "Fine," I lie, and she gives me a look, knowing I'm not.

"How's Fairchild house arrest going?" she inquires.

"Not very well. My grandmother is hovering over me every second she's there. Questioning me about every moment I spend tutoring Rowan. Reminding me every second how horrible his family is and how his two older brothers are nothing but trouble." I pause, my lips pursing as I look over my shoulder at him. His eyes meet mine before I turn back to Zal. "It's exhausting."

"I'm surprised she let you come out tonight."

"Only because Willow promised her I'd be with Paisley the entire time."

"What about the Yuletide Ball next month?"

I shrug. "It's still up in the air if I can go. I mean, I have been grounded for life. In fae years, that is like . . . thousands of years. Besides, I'm not sure I can stomach any more school dances after what happened with Nikki at homecoming."

"What a shame that all was. It was such a beautiful theme, too—Written in the Stars." Zal frowns. "But," she perks up. "The Yuletide Ball will have lit trees, white and clear balloons, elegant confetti, snowflakes . . ." She trails off, getting a dreamy look in her eyes. "It will be a magical winter wonderland. Sans drama, faux blood, and murdering."

"You need to stop volunteering for the decorating committees." I laugh and throw a french fry at her. "Maybe consider joining the debate team with me. It's less bloody and dramatic."

Zal's eyes widen as she looks over my shoulder. "Speaking of drama."

"What?" I ask, turning to see what she is looking at, and then swing back to her quickly.

"Hi, Rowan," Zal chirps, looking amused.

"Ladies," he uses his flirting voice.

I try not to fidget at the sound of his husky voice as he stands next to our table.

My eyes plead with my best friend not to do what I know she is about to.

Zal's eyes jump between me and him. "Well, girls, let's go pick out some songs at the jukebox, shall we?" She pushes Paisley and Makenna out of the booth on the other side, disappearing.

"Hey." I watch as he takes a seat across from me.

"Hey, yourself," he responds dryly.

"What are you doing here this evening?"

"We were hungry, and I understand this is where residents come to eat."

I stare at my plate.

"That is, everyone but you, who comes here to stare at her food."

My gaze darts around the restaurant before falling back to him.

"No one is watching us. Your virtue is safe with me."

Rowan steals a fry off my plate, and I snort because it isn't. It really, *really* isn't safe.

"You and your friends out crooking this evening?" I tease.

He gifts me an amused grin. "Cole isn't part of the Order. And no. Some nights, believe it or not, flannels, we just like to hang out and eat greasy burgers and fries. What about you?"

"I don't steal."

"I thought you were grounded for eternity."

"I am. Paisley is my cousin, so I got a family pass tonight."

I follow his gaze as it slides over my shoulder, landing on Paisley before he leans in and lowers his voice. "Listen, Cole is a jerk. You might want to keep your cousin away from him."

Staring at him, I smile. "Guess it takes one to know one."

"Normally, I would agree with you." He snatches another fry off my plate. "In this instance, he and I are different. I don't walk all over girls and verbally abuse them."

"I'll keep an eye on her," I reply. That doesn't sound like the Cole I know.

He knocks on the table. "I have to go. Sleep tight, flannels."

AFTER BARELY MAKING curfew and dodging my grandmother, I sneak into my bedroom, closing the door behind me. With a slow exhale, I let my human glamour slip. Walking over to my vanity, I flick my wrists, and the twinkle lights around my room come on, bathing me in a soft white light.

My ears stretch and lengthen to their points under my hair, and my face narrows the slightest bit. The fae blood flowing through my veins gives my skin a bright sheen and deepens the purple color of my hair and eyes, making me look much healthier. Less dull. Other than those changes, I look like my human self. I smile at the image reflecting back in the mirror.

For some reason, I always feel much prettier when I am not hiding behind human glamour.

"Fae looks good on you."

My head snaps up and whips around to see Rowan lying on my bed.

"What are you doing in here?" I whisper-shout.

He shrugs. "Since you're grounded, I figured I would come hang out with you."

My mouth threatens to drop at his sudden appearance, but I hold it in check. Lifting my fingers, I release my fae magic, locking my bedroom door. "How did you get in here?"

"Turns out the House of Fairchild isn't as secure as one would think a prison would be."

"Ever been to a shrink?"

"No. Why?"

"I think you might need one."

Rowan settles in, getting comfortable on my pillow just before he waves his hand around.

"Who knew you were so girlie, Jules?"

The sight of him in my bed sends a chill rippling along my skin. "My gran decorated."

"So, none of this pink forest-chic is yours?"

"No. My room at home, in Creekwood, is light gray and lavender. More modern."

"Is anything in here yours?"

"The lights are. Oh, and the lantern on my nightstand is." Rowan goes to touch it, but I screech and jump for it. "My grandfather gave that to me. It can only be touched by fae blood."

Surprise crosses his expression before he puts his hands up in surrender.

"Sorry." I shift on my feet. "It's an heirloom."

"Okay." He nods his understanding.

That's when I notice the green shake that Chef Anne left for me on my nightstand, and I internally groan. I snatch it up and head to the attached bathroom, tossing it down the drain.

My grandmother is convinced a vitamin and mineral intake deficiency is the reason for my recent lack of common sense, as she puts it. What's funny is that for the past month, I've been tossing out the drinks, and I've felt healthier and more myself. Go figure. Although, it could also be Rowan's presence breathing air into my life.

Reentering my room, I put the empty glass back and look down at my pillow. Rowan is smiling up at me, comfortable, and I sigh, realizing he probably isn't going anywhere.

"Why can the lantern only be touched by fae blood?" he asks.

"Why don't you ask me something normal? Like, what is your favorite kind of music, Jules?"

His eyes connect with mine. "I don't need to ask what I already know."

"Which is?"

"Avalanche City is a favorite of yours. I'm guessing you play "Love Love Love" over, and over, and over again." The correct answer falls from his lips as if he pulled it out of thin air.

I bristle. "How did you know that?"

Rowan motions to his left. "Your iPad is sitting on your bed, open to Spotify. And the song is on repeat."

He laughs, and I kneel on the side of my bed, reaching over him to grab my tablet.

"Stop being nosey."

"Hey. You left it open."

"Because it's my room. My space."

When I lean back to stand, Rowan shifts under me, causing me to lose my balance and almost fall onto him. Quickly, he moves, and his arms reach up, preventing me from dropping on top of him. I try to stand up, but his hands form a band of steel around me so I can't release myself from his grip. My long hair tumbles forward, falling in his face as he takes in a steady breath.

"I love that your hair always smelled like flowers," he says, voice low.

"Smelled?" I whisper, and he stiffens.

"Smells," he corrects. "I meant . . . I love that your hair always *smells* like flowers."

I search his face. "Rowan—"

"You need to stop drinking the shakes your grandmother is having made for you."

My brows pinch together. "Why?"

He reaches up and with one hand, brushes the hair away from my face. There is such intensity in his eyes, as if he is willing me to understand what he is trying to nonverbally convey.

"You're always so cryptic," I accuse.

"I can smell rosemary mixed with elder bush in it. There may also be some traces of goofer dust, but I can't be sure because when it's ground, it's hard to detect unless you taste it."

"I don't know what those are."

"Mage spellcasters use elder bush and rosemary to erase good memories. Goofer dust destroys love and relationships," he explains, his eyes turning cold and hard.

I jerk back, but he sits up, following me, taking my face in his palms. "Do you understand me, Jules? You need to stop drinking it. She's purposely making you forget."

"Forget what?" I fire back, scared by the desperation in his voice.

Something flickers over his face. Neither of us look away, but a heavy tension-filled quality settles in the air between us. And for some reason, it makes my heart sink and my stomach drop.

"Me."

The single word makes my breath hitch. Something inside me believes him, even as my mind rebels at the idea. "That's absurd. I know our families have issues, but I am with you every Tuesday and Thursday for tutoring. It's not like she can wipe out my memory of you."

He lets go of me with a curse and rubs his hands down his face.

Keeping quiet, I watch him as he appears to have some sort of internal conversation with himself.

A few minutes later, his tone is soft when he speaks. "Can I try something?"

My gaze slides to the left, but snaps back to him when he puts a finger under my chin.

"Look at me, Jules." He moves his hands back to my cheeks, causing me to still. Gently, his fingers smooth over my face. "Please."

His voice is soul-wrenching with an urgent edge to it.

His expression and his voice, both so sincere, fill me with a deep sense of dread. Whatever he is about to do, or tell me, it is going to change my life, forever. Rowan's gentle stare penetrates me, locking me into place. He seems to be wrestling with what to tell me, or do next.

His lips part as he leans forward, gently bringing my face to his. "I need you to understand."

"Understand what?" I ask, matching his tone.

"This." His voice is barely above a murmur as his thumbs trace circles on my cheeks.

Time slows as I wait for him to show me whatever he's looking for when he searches my gaze. Every quiet moment that stretches between us is torture as he moves closer. Rowan's head slants as he leans in more, his breath fanning over my mouth right before his lips brush against mine.

With a flutter, my lids slide closed as I bask in the tender quality of his soft kiss.

It's innocent, intimate. Not at all what I would have expected from Rowan Bishop.

As he tips my head back and explores my lips, something deep within him reaches inside of me, burning my soul and sending my heart into overdrive. Whatever I'm feeling, I don't ever want it to end. I've been kissed before, but nothing in this world, or any other, compares to this.

When he finally pulls back, I take in an unsteady breath.

"What now?" I whisper across his mouth, dizzy from the intoxication of it all.

"Now, you remember."

Zoning out, I twirl the teal masquerade mask outlined with gold glitter in my hands before placing it back down on the similarly colored invitation sitting on my textbook. I can't concentrate. Apparently, it's a new affliction of mine ever since Rowan's visit. And kiss.

My eyes close, and my lips tingle, recalling the way his soft, warm lips felt as they danced over mine. A text from Mom—saying how excited she is to see me next week—pulls me out of my reverie. My father is being sworn in to the Seelie Court, so my grandmother and I are going to watch him accept his seat. Space from Rowan might be good. Especially since no matter how hard I try, I don't remember anything, leaving me feeling frustrated at our weird conversation.

The chair next to me disappears. Without a word, Rowan drops in it and pushes it forward, reappearing by my side. With a quick side-glance, I take him in. His hair is tousled and messy, and there are shadows under his eyes. He looks as tired as I feel. I return my focus to the pile of stuff in front of me, but I can feel his stare on me. It's like every cell in my body is aware of him.

"Where have you been? Tutoring was supposed to start fifteen minutes ago," I snarl.

"Order business."

Unable to stop myself, I turn toward him. When our eyes lock, the air between us jumps, filled with heat and electricity. Magic. The last time I saw him, we were kissing.

And now, I have no idea where we stand.

"Everything okay?" I ask, not really caring about his secret society.

He reaches out and with one hand and runs his fingers over my cheek. "It is now."

I take in a deep breath and let it out slowly. "I got your invitation. Or should I say Romeo's?"

A wry grin twists his lips. He leans closer, and my entire body relaxes at the warm energy he's creating. "The Order is throwing me a masquerade birthday bash for my eighteenth birthday."

"So I read." I yawn and try to focus on him. "It also says to be there promptly at nine o'clock in the evening." I slur my words. "I'm not sure I'm ready for a visit to the House of Bishop yet."

Rowan arches a brow at me. "Are you okay?

I push away the dizzy feeling that is taking over. "Fine."

"Okay," he responds, sounding unconvinced. "So, are you coming?"

"I'll try. I am still grounded." My eyelids suddenly feel heavy and hard to keep open.

He leans in even more. His scent surrounds me. I try to push back, but he reaches out, taking hold of my arm. Underneath his touch, pleasant tingles run over my skin.

Heat suddenly floods my veins. We're too close, and there is too much tension between us. It's suffocating. When Rowan's gaze burns into mine, I forget how to breathe. All of a sudden, my lungs have stopped working, and a strange fog clouds my brain. I feel myself sway, and in the far-off distance, I can hear Rowan curse under his breath before everything goes black.

My eyelids flutter open, and immediately I have to squint and raise my hands to shield my eyes from the sunshine beaming down on me. Confused, I sit up and look around, noticing I'm in a field filled with purple wildflowers. The same one Rowan took us to that day in the mountains, near the falls.

Children laughing in the distance pull my attention as I look around until I see them. A boy around nine and a girl around the same age approach me. Narrowing my eyes, I stretch my head closer when I realize the little girl is me. What in the world? I stay quiet as they run closer, now in front of me.

"Why am I always chasing you, Julianna Fairchild?" the boy stops and asks, slightly out of breath.

The younger version of me turns and faces him.

With her hands on her hips, she tilts her head. "Are you saying I'm not worth chasing?"

The boy smirks wickedly at her. "Just let me catch you. At least once in my lifetime."

"No."

"Why not?"

"'Cause if you do," she frowns, "you'll stop chasing me."

The boy's brows raise. "Jules." I shiver at the familiar way he says her name. My name. "I won't ever stop chasing you. You're my best friend." He takes her hand in his. "I promise."

She steps closer. "No matter what?"

"No matter what."

"What if I am on Tír na nÓg for the summer?" she whispers.

"Then, I'll use the lantern your grandfather guards and enter the portal to find you!" he promises.

"What if we are older and my parents make us move to California or someplace else?"

He steps closer to her. "Wherever you are, Jules, I will chase after you and find you."

"What if you leave?" She pouts.

"Then I will come back for you," he swears.

"Promise?" Her eyes brighten.

"I double infinity promise." He lifts his sleeve, and she holds out her wrist.

My lips part when I see the two of them have double infinity tattoos on their wrist and forearm.

Just like Rowan and I do.

The boy presses his tattoo to the girl's. "I double infinity promise."

"I double infinity promise, too."

When she isn't looking, he places a quick, chaste kiss on her lips.

With wide, awestruck eyes, she stares at him. "What was that for, Rowan Bishop?"

"So you will always remember me." He winks and runs in the opposite direction.

The girl turns and looks at me before whispering, "Inamorata."

WITH A STARTLE, my eyes pop open, and I draw in a shallow breath. After a few blinks, I see Rowan's face hovering over me with a worried expression etched into it. I try pushing away from him, but he reaches out, taking hold of my upper arms in a light grip. His expression is worried as his eyes latch onto mine, and I forget how to breathe. He was the boy in my memory.

Flashes of memories flood over me, running through my mind like a movie. Images of us playing as small children. Dancing in the field under the stars. Laying in the grass as he read to me, with the sunshine warming us. Me sitting alone in the field, with the rain falling on me, when he left. My family and his, promising me it would be okay before everything went blank.

Fascinated, I watch his lips as he speaks. It's hard to pay attention to his words when I realize that we've known and loved each other our entire lives.

Before they took him away from me.

Somehow Rowan's voice makes it through the strange fog clouding my brain.

"Jules. Are you okay?" he asks, sounding worried.

I stare at his lips when he says my nickname.

I knew he was familiar.

In the core of my soul, I knew that I knew him.

He moves closer, his hands sliding up my arm and resting at the back of my neck, slowly weaving them through the strands of loose hair. And my lips part as an unexpected ache fills me.

An ache that was buried and hidden from me presents itself again deep within my heart. An ache that ignited when they took him from me. Tension fills me as I'm unsure of what I'm feeling.

"Inamorata," I whisper.

Rowan's brows furrow. "What?"

"It means love in Italian. My grandfather used to call my grandmother his inamorata."

"Okay."

"I remember," I blow out, and his eyes widen as he swallows.

Two simple words. That's all they are, but the weight and meaning behind them are huge.

"You. The field we played in as small children. We got matching tattoos because we always had to double infinity promise each other. It was your idea, so we wouldn't have to say it all the time," I ramble on one long drawn-out breath. "My first kiss. My first love. It was you."

Rowan watches me for a moment. His top teeth pull in his lip ring as his fingers brush over my cheek, tucking a strand of hair behind my ear. There is an unexpected softness in his eyes, and I have to swallow the lump in my throat. Suddenly I'm overcome with emotion.

Years of repressed feelings for him hit me all at once, and I'm swimming in sensations.

Without thought, I grab his face and pull him toward me, kissing him. There wasn't a moment of hesitation. His mouth was on mine and mine on his. Rowan shudders and releases a sound from the back of his throat like a half growl, half moan. Shivers of pleasure tickle my skin at the sound, and I stop thinking when he deepens the kiss to the kind that leaves little room for thought. Raw sensations swim over me, and after a long time, our kisses slow, becoming tender and something more emotional and real. When we finally pull away, I'm breathless and dazed.

"Wow," I exhale.

"What?" he whispers across my lips.

"That was better than I remember," I murmur. "It feels different."

Rowan releases a dark chuckle. "That's because I know what I'm doing now."

CHAPTER 9

*M*y throat constricts when Rowan walks over to the window bench I am sitting on. He moves with an unsettling silence and swiftness. Passing me a glass of water, he takes a seat across from me, and this time, when he looks at me, a slow burn makes its way up my cheeks. How could I not remember him and all that we've shared? He positions himself so his body is angled slightly toward mine, our knees mere inches apart.

"How did we get here?" I look around my bedroom.

"When you blacked out, I did a travel spell to bring us here. I figured it was better than having you pass out in the library and us causing a small scene," he speaks with confidence.

"You used magic? In public, again?" I accused.

He flashes his cocky smile at me. "And we left campus." He winks. "Are you okay?"

"I'm not sure. This is all so overwhelming." My gaze slides out the window as I take in the star-filled night sky. "You're going to have to fill in the blanks here for me. From the beginning."

"Our mothers were friends, believe it or not. Secret friends." His voice is low but firm.

"You're telling me my mom was friends with the Bishop boys' mom?" I challenge.

Heat spreads to my face. A sick feeling forms in my stomach when I realize how it sounded.

"Roman and Ronan share the same mother. But I don't. My mother is," he pauses.

"Is what?"

"Part of the Unseelie Court." He watches my reaction as I nearly choke on a sip of water.

He's joking, I tell myself, but the look on his face is void of humor.

The Seelie Court are light fae. We are known for our good nature and kindness toward nature and humanity. The Unseelie Court consists of the dark-inclined fae. Given my family's status, I find it hard to believe that my mother would befriend an Unseelie Court member.

I feel Rowan's gaze on me, making my pulse quicken and my insides twist and roll around.

Then again . . . my own argument dies on my lips as I look at him.

That means Rowan is half Unseelie, mixed with his father's mage blood, which would explain why he's more powerful than either of his two brothers. Why they sent him away.

"Go on," I encourage him, and take another shaky sip of water, needing something to do.

"My mother was my father's mistress for many years. When she became pregnant, she turned to your mom for support. Given our families' history here in Havenwood Falls, and seats on opposing fae courts, they kept their friendship a secret. They vowed that their children would be friends, regardless of the difference in our fae bloodlines, or the feud between the families we were born into," he continues. "We've known one another since birth," he points out.

"You were born in November," I think out loud. "My birthday is in January."

He averts his gaze. A coolness falls across his expression, which sends chills down my spine.

"We'll both be eighteen," he states, then quickly shakes off whatever was bothering him.

At his mood change, my defenses shoot back up, and I press my lips together.

"What happened? Why did you get sent away and my memory of you wiped out?"

"During the Seelie and Unseelie war, the fae courts discovered our mothers' friendship and put an end to it. For what reason, I have no idea. My mother never told me. Regardless, the mandate trickled down to our life here in Havenwood Falls. Your grandfather, father, and my father all discovered their friendship when our mothers were brought in front of the fae courts. The moment they saw our tattoos and learned of our feelings for one another . . ." He pauses, holding my eyes. "I mean friendship. Everyone decided it all had to stop."

"Stop how?" I ask.

"The fae courts ruled that both my mother and I return to Unseelie—but Roman stepped in. He didn't want me growing up around the Unseelie Court. So he offered to send me away to boarding school, vowing that he would alter my existence here in town with a spell. Somewhere in all their agreements, the Court of the Sun and the Moon allowed me to be an exception to the town's memory wards. I guess it didn't sit well with them that an eleven-year old kid would be released into the world with no past or family ties."

"That's insane," I blow out.

"Roman visited often and once a year checked in with the Court, confirming I was adhering to their rules. The Fairchilds agreed to it all, even your mother, as long as you remained in town with them and had your memory altered. Roman ensured your family was supplied with the memory herbs to help you forget—"

"You?" I finish for him with a sharp look.

"Me," he confirms.

I flush under his steady gaze. His face darkens as his eyes lock on mine. He moves in closer, stopping only inches from my face. I sit forward, placing my water down. I will not let what happened in the past control my life, and I certainly am not going to run and hide from it now.

"They all made a fatal mistake," I whisper.

"What's that?" he asks through clenched teeth.

"You promised to come back for me," I remind him.

He stares me down in silence, making my heart flutter. Rowan looks like he is seriously debating with himself about whether or not to confirm the vision I saw when I blacked out.

"I've always kept my promises to you, Jules."

"That's why you got kicked out of all those schools? So you could eventually come back?"

His eyes hold mine with a steady, critical gaze that I can't really decipher. "I did it so there was no other choice but to return. It took me eight schools before I was allowed to come back," he speaks softly. "I had to promise to stay away from you, but—"

My fingers move nervously as I take his face between my hands. "But what?"

He's silent for a moment. "I couldn't."

Something changes between us at his admission. My heart picks up speed, and a flood of emotions washes over me. Everything I have ever felt for him grips me. I try to ignore it because my mind still has to catch up with what my heart and body are feeling. Adrenaline flies through my veins when his thumb lifts and runs over the tattoo on my wrist. His touch sends heat and want through me. I close my eyes and take in a slow breath, trying to calm myself.

"Now what? What if they find out that I remember?" I reopen my eyes.

"They won't."

Fear makes these next words crawl from my throat. "How can you be sure?"

The tension is thick between us. I can feel it resonating off him, crashing into me.

"I'm supposed to go to Tír na nÓg with my grandmother for Thanksgiving through New Year's for my father's induction to the Seelie Court. The Court of the Sun and the Moon and school already approved it. What if they discover I remember you and wipe away my memories while I'm there?" I try not to panic, but given my newfound recollection of feelings, it's hard.

In a blink, Rowan moves closer so I can feel his warm breath on my face. He looks back and forth to each of my eyes, his brows furrowing, as if he's trying to understand something.

"Hey." He slides his hands into my hair, dropping his forehead to mine. Rowan's gaze never leaves mine. "I know what I'm doing. I have a plan to protect us. You just need to trust and believe in me." He searches my eyes. "Can you do that?"

I let out a shaky breath. "What's the plan?"

A loud knock at the door has us jumping apart and Rowan cursing under his breath.

"Julianna? Are you in there?" My grandmother's voice cuts through the wood.

My eyes widen, and Rowan's blazing eyes find mine. Our stares lock, and his expression calms. He points to my closet before silently making his way over to it to hide inside. Once the door is closed, I take in a calm breath and slowly open my bedroom door.

"I'm here." I manage not to sound as nervous as I feel.

Miss Mary Beth walks in, taking in my room, looking around before her gaze settles on me.

"Your instructor at the Academy called and said you missed this evening's class."

"Oh, um." I shake my head. "Yeah. I was just tired after tutoring. That's all."

"Tired?" She steps to me, placing her hand on my forehead. "Are you feeling all right? You never miss a class. That is so unlike you, Jules. You are taking your vitamin shakes, right?"

"I'm fine, Gran." I tilt my head away from her, desperately wanting her to leave.

She frowns. "Are you sure? You have been acting strange lately. And you're flushed."

"I'm just tired. And missing Mom and Dad," I lie.

Her lips press together. "Well, it will be good for us to go spend some time with them when you're off for winter break. Get you out of town for a bit. Refresh your focus and fae energy on the island . . ." Her voice trails off.

"It will," I agree.

"I'll have Chef Anne make you some tea to help you relax before bed."

"Thanks." I force a smile.

My grandmother stares at me with a strange, confused look on her face before she shakes it off and places her smile back on her lips. "If you need anything, I'll be at the country club tonight for a Historical Society meeting, but tomorrow we'll have breakfast."

"Sounds good."

"Get some rest." She cups my cheek before stepping around me and closing the door.

Blowing out a long breath, I watch as Rowan slides out of the closet. The shadows following him make him seem dangerous and dark. How did I never pick up on his Unseelie blood before?

His gaze is intense as he steps in front of me. "Find a way to come to my birthday."

"Okay," I promise as his eyes dip to my lips, and he leans into my space.

The rush of sensations that Rowan's look sends across my body is both scary and thrilling.

"Guess what I found in your closet?" he whispers with a wicked edge.

"What?" I ask, breathless, wanting nothing more than for his lips to brush mine.

Rowan holds up a pair of flannel pajamas.

ZALTANA STUDIES me in a way that has me feeling transparent. I blink rapidly as she finishes applying the tiny decorations next to my right eye. Leaning back, she inspects her work. In all honesty, I have mixed feelings about letting her do my makeup. She tends to have a heavy artist's hand when she creates magic, as she likes to say.

"There." She smiles. "The gold color looks amazing on you!"

I hold back an eye roll at her overexcited state before spinning to look in my mirror.

The tiny golden leaves she designed around my eyes really do look super cool. I smile and thank her, taking in the stunning peacock feathers in teal she designed around hers. They match the short, strapless dress she's wearing, embroidered in the front with peacock feathers.

"All right, so . . ." She flutters around me. "Let's get our story straight for your grandmother."

I watch her in the vanity. "She's not here."

"Where is she?"

"The Historical Society is meeting again at the country club to discuss plans for the Festival of Lights. Gran's totally focused on finalizing the details before we leave for the fae realm."

My best friend frowns. "I hate that you're going to be gone for an entire month."

"Me, too." I avert my eyes, knowing I am going to miss her . . . and Rowan.

"I'm surprised the powers that be approved you missing more school than just break." She puts her makeup art brushes in her case. "Or that your grandmother allowed you to go tonight."

"As for tonight, Gran thinks I'm going out with you and Paisley and staying at Willow's." I shrug. "The Court had something to do with school. Elsmed," I add.

Zaltana nods her understanding as she stands to her full height. The high heels she is wearing make her seem even taller and more supermodel-like than she is. She gives me a critical once-over.

"What?"

"Are you sure you want to do this?" she asks, knowing what is happening between Rowan and me. I filled her in on one of our recent shopping trips, and since then, she's become overprotective.

"Sneak out to a masquerade ball?" I arch my eyebrow. "Sure, why not?"

"I don't mean that. I mean, whatever it is Rowan has planned. Are you sure you trust him? Especially after finding out he's Unseelie?" She pins me with a look. "Why didn't he just tell you all this, if it was true? Why did he string you along and try to get you to remember?"

"I can't explain it, Zal, but I trust Rowan." I take her hand and squeeze. "I swear."

"You're my best friend. I just don't want you getting hurt, Jules."

"I know."

"And Rowan Bishop, well, he seems like dark, dangerous trouble. The kind of trouble that, when it cuts and wounds you, is deep and painful. The kind of pain that you don't just heal from."

I stand and hug her. "Then it's good I have a Native American healer as my best friend."

With a long, hard squeeze, she holds me for a moment before pulling back. "I'm afraid the kind of hurt that Rowan will inflict on you is the kind that even I can't heal for you, my friend."

My long teal and gold satin one-shoulder dress floats around me as I stand in the doorway of the Bishop estate. When I bend my knee, it peeks out of the long slit on the right side. The gray stone mansion is lit and decorated in the colors of the Order, making it look and feel less eerie.

I wobble on the heels I'm wearing as Zal and I make our way into the foyer and take in all the decorations and guests dressed in gowns or tuxedos, wearing their masks. Large gold drapes hang between archways, leading guests into the magnificent Bishop ballroom, which is backlit in teal and gold. Masks hang from candelabras in the center of round tables. It's all so elaborate and breathtaking.

Music pumps from a loud sound system, the DJ on display to the right of the dance floor. Bars and food are to the left. One thing is for sure —when Roman and Ronan are away, Rowan knows how to throw a party. Zal grabs my arm to get my attention.

"Hey, I think I see River."

"How do you know?" I ask, since everyone is masked.

"Oh, I know." Her voice becomes seductive. "Mind if I go say hi, really quick?"

"Go. I'll be fine."

"Are you sure?"

"Yes. I'll see you later." I wink.

Zal waves her cell phone at me. "Constant communication. All night."

"I promise."

After some time spent mingling with friends and my cousin, I look around the dance floor, wondering where Zal went off to. Circling the room, I come to a complete standstill.

Rowan's bathed in the flickering glow of candlelight, watching me.

In typical Rowan fashion, he's not wearing a tux or a mask. Instead, he's wearing black jeans, a black T-shirt, and a black velvet blazer that, when the light hits it just right, gives off a teal sheen. His stare on me is so concentrated that without even considering what I'm doing, I step toward him, holding his eye contact as he magnetically pulls me in.

A craving to be wrapped in his arms unfurls deep within me, the kind of feeling you can't force or replicate. The kind that just is. When your soul knows it belongs to someone else.

When I'm finally in front of him, Rowan's gaze slides over me as he leans toward me.

I watch him through my mask. "Happy birthday, Romeo."

"For I never saw true beauty till this night," he quotes Shakespeare, smiling down at me.

"Speaking of Romeo and Juliet." I smirk and hand him the gift I've been holding. Eyeing me, he unwraps the DVD. "It's the good one with Leonardo DiCaprio. And, for the record, I stole it."

He cocks his pierced brow at me. "You stole, flannels? Isn't that against the law?"

"Crooked. From Zal's bedroom shelf. And consider my thieving part of your gift."

"Thank you." Placing the DVD on the table next to us, he looks at me. "Dance with me."

I don't say anything as he wraps one arm around my waist, the other taking hold of my hand. The music slows as a haunting melody swirls around us.

I stare up into Rowan's deep navy gaze holding mine so tenderly. The blood rushes through my body as he pulls me closer, and we begin to sway. When the lights reflect in his hair, my breath escapes me. It's in this moment I realize what I've been feeling for him this entire time is love. One look at him and my whole life seems to make sense.

He smiles down at me, and shivers run through me.

The hand resting above my hip shifts, and the skin under my dress heats.

"You look beautiful," he whispers in my ear, and I find it hard to breathe.

His cheek brushes over mine, and a dizzying rush of sensations flies through me. After a while, I close my eyes and lean my cheek against his jacket, sinking into his arms. Being with him like this—there is no way to describe it. It's peaceful. Right. This isn't a crush or fleeting moment, it's deeper. Rowan is my fate. My soul's other half. And when he holds me, he creates our own perfect bubble, away from all the prying eyes that are watching us right now.

As the song winds down, his fingers brush over my cheek, tucking a strand of hair behind my ear. "Come on," he whispers.

I lift my head to find an unexpected softness in his eyes. I don't argue. I let him lead me away from the party, the music and lights. Because truth be told, wherever Rowan Bishop leads me, I'll follow him. Seconds later, he pulls me into a dark, private alcove in the hallway. It's such a small space that there isn't much room to move around, and before I can say anything, his jaw grazes my cheek, followed by his lips.

The touches were quick, but I find it hard to breathe nonetheless.

Rowan lowers his head, our mouths nearly touching. His breath is warm, intoxicating.

Even in the dark, I see his gaze drop to my lips, and my heart flips in my chest. Neither of us move for what seems like an eternity, caught in a daze before he gently removes my mask.

"I want to take you somewhere." His voice is husky.

"Let's go," I reply.

CHAPTER 10

*W*hen I put my dress on and let Zal spend hours on my makeup and hair tonight, I had no idea I would be riding on the back of Rowan's motorcycle. I make a gruff sound in my throat as I stare at his bike in the garage with skepticism. Is he serious that he wants me to ride on this now?

"You aren't suddenly scared of my bike, are you?" he asks, swinging his leg over it.

"Hardly. It's just . . ." I motion to my dress. "I'm not really dressed for riding tonight."

Rowan looks over his shoulder, his eyes taking me in. With a dark chuckle, he slides off it and approaches me, holding my eyes with a wicked edge to his smile. With a quick motion, the sound of the dress material ripping echoes around the garage. My gaze drops to the skirt, which he's destroyed. The extra material is pooled on the floor, exposing my legs. I stare at them in disbelief for a few seconds before looking back at him and narrowing my eyes. The cool air floats up the small amount of material covering my lower body, causing me to shiver.

"Now, straddle my bike, flannels," he orders, handing me a helmet and waiting.

Annoyed, I grab the helmet from him, shaking my head at it with a questioning look, since he didn't have one for me on our previous ride up to the field. "New purchase?" I question.

He shrugs. "You said it was really hard to get brain splatter off the road."

With a smile on my lips, I put it on and swing my leg over his Harley.

Rowan's eyes darken when he takes me in, sitting on his bike, before he joins me.

"Hold on," he commands.

I grab onto his waist and try to ignore the raw electricity I feel as our bodies press together. Swallowing, I lean forward. "You owe me two hundred dollars for the dress."

The garage door opens, and Rowan starts his bike, driving us forward. The freezing Colorado wind whips at my face and turns my bare legs into ice cubes as he tears down the road. Within seconds, his warm magic bubble surrounds us.

His body feels like heaven against mine. I've come to learn there is nothing more exhilarating than being plastered against Rowan on his motorcycle.

Driving as fast as he does has us arriving at our destination way too soon. He pulls into a dark alley that runs between two buildings. Once we're parked, Rowan shifts, and when his warm body slides off the bike, I immediately feel a loss at the separation.

Taking off my helmet, I look around.

Rowan grabs my hand and pulls me toward the street, making a hard left. We walk up a flight of stairs to a door on the second floor, and I try not to fall back down them with my heels. A closed sign greets us, and I frown at it before reading the writing on the glass door, Tragic Ink.

"On your birthday, you wanted to take me to a tattoo studio?" I question, confused.

He doesn't answer me, taking out his cell and shooting off a quick text.

Within seconds, a woman comes to the glass door. She has short blond hair and deep green eyes, and her pale skin is covered in tattoos. She opens the door and with a sense of urgency, ushers us in, giving us a no-nonsense attitude. Once we enter the studio, we follow her to the back, and she turns on one small light. Immediately, I sense her fae blood, but it doesn't help me relax.

"You're late," the woman states.

"Is everything ready, Gwen?" Rowan's tone is clipped and tight.

"Of course," Gwen bites out. "The question is, will I still do it?"

"Do what?" I interrupt.

Gwen's eyes narrow on me. "Is she even eighteen, Rowan?"

"Yes," he lies, but Gwen pins him with a disbelieving look. "In January."

Gwen releases several curses before I interrupt her rant. "What exactly is going on here?"

Rowan rubs his face. "Julianna, this is Gwen Facharro. She owns Tragic Ink," Rowan introduces. "Gwen has agreed to do us a favor."

"More like blackmailed," she counters.

I force a smile at the woman shooting daggers at me. "I don't need another tattoo."

Rowan steps in front of me, blocking my view of Gwen. "We're not here for new tattoos, Jules. Gwen's ink is capable of something," he pauses, "magical."

I can feel the animosity oozing off Gwen as Rowan takes a moment to explain things to me.

"Gwen is going to go over our double infinity tattoos, infusing the ink with magic. The magic will provide a safety barrier, blocking anyone who tries to wipe our memories again."

"Clock's ticking," Gwen says, like we're an aggravating nuisance.

"Just—" I squeeze Rowan's elbow, dragging him into a corner. "One second."

Gwen rolls her eyes but busies herself cleaning, giving us a bit of privacy.

"Her unfriendly bedside manner aside, how do you know we can trust her?" I ask him.

Rowan's body is tense as he focuses on me. "You just have to trust me on this one, Jules."

The strain in his voice is putting me on edge. My eyes slide over to Gwen. Her name sounds familiar but I don't know where I've heard of her before. "I don't know."

"Listen, I overheard my brother, Roman, talking to his . . . whatever she is," he exhales.

"She?"

"Ada. Ada was telling Roman about Gwen's special fae gifts. She can magically infuse the tattoos she creates. I thought maybe she could help us. When I first reached out to her, she denied her gifts. But then, when I lied and said Ada sent me, she hesitated but agreed to help us.

"Gwen is fae. I trust her." He lowers his voice. "You are leaving tomorrow, for over a month, to go to the Seelie realm. Surrounded by the Court. I need to know your memory is protected."

The way his words hang between us finalizes my resolve.

I bite my bottom lip. "She seems unfriendly."

"Look," Gwen interrupts, seeming irritated. "I'm not very polite. Blame it on my upbringing. That said, I can help you two lovebirds. If I infuse your tattoos with magic, I can produce a protection shield from either of you having your memory wiped out again. The magic I gift, though, expires once you use it up, so be sure to only call upon it if you absolutely need it."

I tilt my head at Rowan, giving him my unamused look.

His eyes plead with me, and I give in.

"I guess it's worth a shot," I concede.

I take a seat in the chair, showing Gwen my wrist. She quickly inspects the tattoo and then goes into another room to grab what she needs. When she does, Rowan takes off his jacket and throws it to the side. My eyes wander over him.

Straddling a stool next to me, he slides his palm over my other hand. "This is going to work."

"It's your birthday. Shouldn't I be the one giving you a gift?"

"You already have. You remembered. And, well, it's everything."

My lips twitch into a smile at the meaning behind his words.

Moments later, Gwen returns and gets everything ready.

Just as she is about to start, I meet her hard gaze. "I've never infused a pre-existing design with my magic, so this is new. For all of us," she points out before the buzzing sound begins.

"Wait," I stop her. "Never?"

"I don't just give out magic. So, if you tell anyone, I will deny it. But for Ada," she stops herself and waits for me to settle back in. "Just don't go sending your friends in here."

"We understand," Rowan assures her.

An hour later, both our tattoos look less dull, but the same. Gwen lotions them and adds the plastic protective covers before we pay her, and she reminds us again to keep this quiet.

After a short ride, the sound of tires sliding over gravel as Rowan's motorcycle comes to a stop in front of his family estate has me sighing, not really wanting to go back to the party.

It's getting late, and I still need to pack for my trip to Tír na nÓg tomorrow.

Taking in the throngs of kids mulling around, drinking witch's brew and acting like fools, I wrap my arms tighter around Rowan, basking in his warmth.

As if knowing what I'm thinking, he maneuvers us back into the garage, and for a moment, neither of us moves. Closing my eyes, I take in a deep breath, allowing his scent to calm me.

Sadness floats over me. Before tonight, I hadn't given much thought to the fact that I'm not going to see him for an entire month. A sinking feeling makes its way into my stomach. The idea of not being with him hurts. He makes me feel whole. Safe. Wanted. Cherished.

"Hey," he whispers, and watches me ungracefully climb off his bike. "You okay?"

Silently, I keep my eyes on him. Rowan's hair is messy and ruffled from the ride in this unbelievably hot way. I breathe in deeply and try not to show him how nervous he makes me feel, or how my body tingles every time I see him. Now that I've finally admitted to myself how I feel about him, I'm afraid with each look and movement I make, it seeps from me. Taking off the helmet, I nervously run my hands through my tangled hair, trying to smooth it down.

Rowan studies me as my head and heart are at war. I want to dive into him—he's comfort, safety, and pure intrigue all rolled into one amazingly gorgeous package. When his eyes roam over me, it's done with a look that makes my knees weak.

Slowly, he slides off his motorcycle and walks toward me. His expression becomes serious as he studies my face. His body stiffens when I'm a sliver away. Nervous, since I've never done anything like this, I place my palms on his chest and peer up at him through my lashes. My limited experience with my own feelings has me unsure of what to say or how to act.

"I. Um . . . "

"What?" His voice is so husky, I tremble.

The weight of the tension between us echoes in the silence of the garage.

"I don't want to go back to the party," I say, my voice quiet but strong.

Our eyes lock, and I hold my breath when I see his gaze burning with ravenous hunger. The look makes my heart stutter and my head swirl. He moves toward me with a steady intensity, stopping just before our lips meet. With a gentle touch, he slides his fingers over my cheeks.

"No?"

His fingers touch my jaw and slither down, softly tracing the contours of my neck until he reaches the strap on my dress. My eyes close as I drown in the pleasure of his touch.

"No," I whisper.

His thumb sweeps gingerly across my bottom lip, causing my lips to part.

"Are you sure, Julianna?" he asks. "Are you sure you're ready? And want this with me?"

My eyes flutter open and see him staring down at me. For a brief time, we stay still, lost in everything we are feeling but aren't saying. A yearning settles deeper in my body with each passing moment. Without rushing, he slides his hands up and cups my face. His concentration is intense as he stares at my lips, lowering his slowly to mine, causing me to ache for his touch.

"I need to hear you say it," he whispers across my mouth.

A burst of desire ripples through my body, sparking an intense passion that seems to overtake me. There is nothing more I want in the world than to be his, completely.

When his lips brush mine, my own burn like fire. The taste of his mouth spurs an endless need for him. The kiss starts slow as we take in one another, but it quickly intensifies. I move my hands through his hair as he breathes me in, bringing us closer. His hands fall from my face and grip my waist, pressing me closer to him. We stay like this, exploring each other for the longest time, before we reluctantly release each other's lips but don't separate. We're frozen, breathing heavily.

Rowan's voice is deep and lined with need. "Are you sure?" he asks again.

"I want to be yours, in every way possible," I reply, breathlessly.

THE HARSH LIGHT of the morning sun beams through Rowan's open windows. I squint and bury my face in his chest. At the shift, the arm he has around my waist tightens, keeping me glued to him. I lay here, my breath in my throat as memories of last night roll through my mind.

All the intimate moments we shared cause a blush to caress my cheeks. I squeeze my eyes shut. Every inch of me is now hyperaware of him. For the slightest second, embarrassment floods me. Trying not to wake Rowan, I attempt to escape, but he rolls us so I'm on my back, stopping me. His face burrows into the space between my neck and shoulder. His warm breath dances over my skin as he nuzzles the area, causing goosebumps to form on my skin.

Rowan lifts his head, his eyes pooled with the deepest shade of navy as he stares down at me.

"Hi," I whisper.

A sly grin appears on his lips. "Hi."

I swallow when his hand inches up across my stomach, causing my pulse to fly off the charts.

The tips of his fingers brush my ribs, and he lowers his mouth to mine, taking my lips with a soft and gentle kiss. Using his arms, he lifts himself up, hovering over me as we slow our kiss.

His eyes never leave mine as something unspoken and heavy passes between us.

"You okay?" he asks, his voice rough and sleepy sounding.

"Yeah," I say, barely recognizing my own voice.

With a final kiss to my lips, he disappears from above me.

I stay where I am, staring at the ceiling with my heart pounding. Rolling over, I bury my face in his pillow, breathing in, because it smells like Rowan.

After a few minutes, the door to his bathroom opens, and Rowan strolls out wearing flannel bottoms and no shirt. His hair is messy, and he looks thoroughly sexy. He smiles down at me, sitting on the edge of the bed.

"I like your pajama bottoms," I tease.

A chuckle falls out of him. "I thought you might. Are you hungry?"

I slide my gaze to his clock. "A little. But I have to go."

Rowan's expression falls. "What time are you leaving?"

"Two. But I have tons of packing to do. Besides, I need to get back. My grandmother thinks I stayed at Willow's last night, and if she finds out I didn't, I'll be grounded for two lifetimes."

Rowan lifts the back of his hand, running it over my cheek. "A month without you sucks."

I hold his eyes. "I'm sure you will find plenty of trouble to get into."

"Yeah." He winks. "Probably. But nothing like what we did last night."

I laugh and then cringe at the sound. It sounded choked and ugly. Forced.

Rowan peers down at me. "Being with you . . . it was amazing."

"Yeah?"

"Yeah. I fought for years to get back to you, Jules. A month is nothing."

My heart soars at his statement. "I should get going. Can I shower before I go?"

"Yeah, of course. There are some clothes and girlie products in my bathroom for you."

My eyes widen. "You got me girlie products?"

"It wasn't intentional. Zaltana left them up here during the party last night in case you two wanted to freshen up or change at some point," he explains.

"Ah. Makes more sense." I sit up and plant a gentle kiss on his lips. "Thank you."

"You're welcome. I'll be downstairs. Come down when you're ready."

TWENTY MINUTES LATER, I run my fingers through my damp hair and change into the clothes Zal left for me. I make my way down the curled staircase to find Rowan. When I hear his voice coming from a front room, I smile and begin to make my way over to him, but a second voice stops me. At the conspiring tones being used, I push myself against a wall and listen.

"By the disheveled looks of you this morning, little brother, I'd say our plan was successful?"

"Everything went according to plan, Ronan. The lantern is with the Order."

"Excellent," Ronan replies. "Does she suspect anything?"

"No. And I want to keep her in the dark about this. Jules doesn't need to know we took it."

Closing my eyes, I try to make sense of the conversation. Did he take my grandfather's lantern? And if so, why? My heart falls when I realize that Ronan said plan. At the idea that Rowan used me last night to steal the lantern, my stomach rolls, and I begin to panic. What the hell is going on here? I scoot closer to the doorway, but both of the brothers are gone. I stare into the empty room as thoughts tumble around in my head. Hurt rises so quickly inside me that it leaves me dizzy and almost numb. How could he do this? Use me like this?

He must know what the lantern does and what it means.

A guttural, agitated noise bubbles out of me. I shove the hurt away, feeling so zapped of energy—and pride—that I can barely even stand up. With tears threatening to sting my eyes, I quickly make my way to the front door. Pushing it open, I step into the fresh air, and with one final glance back, I tell myself that everything my family has said about the Bishops is true.

Lies, secrets, and betrayals rule the Bishop boys.

Zal was right. The cut that Rowan has caused isn't one that will ever heal.

Lifting my chin, I walk away from the House of Bishop.

From Rowan.

And from whatever fate once had in store for us.

CHAPTER 11

J stare into the inky sky, lit with a thousand lanterns. The Festival of Lights has always been one of my favorite events in Havenwood Falls. It's designed to remember those supernatural beings who lost their lives in the great massacre. The humans just think it's a cool event every January—they don't understand the true meaning and symbolism behind it. It's a shame.

"You look different," Zal comments from my left.

"I do not."

"Your hair is longer."

"It is not." I roll my eyes at her.

"Your eyes are a deeper shade of violet. It must have been the fae water."

"They are not. Stop it."

"You've been gone for six weeks. I've missed you. This town is boring without you."

"We talked every day." I laugh at my best friend. "Besides, time passes differently in Faerie. So for me, it felt like only a week."

"Still, it was only supposed to be a month in *this* realm, over the holiday break."

I groan. "You know why I stayed longer."

The minute I got home after overhearing Rowan and his brother, I called Zal. She was immediately by my side, consoling me and vowing to murder him, or at least to afflict him with an ancient Native American curse. Something I wouldn't put past her, given the Ute's history of placing curses on witches. Too emotionally drained to give her my approval, I simply told her I needed space and time to figure things out. It was good I spent the holidays with my mom and dad after his induction into the Seelie Court. It reminded me of my goals and focus.

Rowan Bishop had become a distraction from both. I need to finish out the school year and leave Havenwood Falls for college. Be done with all the crazy in this town. Focus on the future.

Zaltana's gaze remains on the lanterns floating in the night sky when she speaks. "Have you talked to Rowan?" she asks with caution. "I've seen him around and he looks . . ."

"He looks like what?"

"Rough, Jules. He looks like someone kicked his puppy."

"Good," I snap out. "Any luck with River?"

She studies me for a moment, looking a bit taken aback at my cruelty. "No. River is tight-lipped about the Order. I've tried to get information about the lantern, but he's all secretive."

"Figures. Everyone in this town either hates or protects the Bishop Boys," I mutter.

"You're starting to sound like your grandmother," Zal points out.

"Well, she's right. They are nothing but trouble."

Zal's lips part, and she narrows her eyes at me.

"What?"

"I never thought I would see the day when you actually agreed with Miss Mary Beth."

I stare at my best friend, then shift my focus to the throngs of people above us on the snow-covered mountain. Zal's right. I hate that I sound like my grandmother. When I first arrived at Tír na nÓg, I was devastated. I couldn't even get out of bed. I refused to speak. My parents were so worried about me. Then the devastation slowly subsided, leaving hurt, frustration, and anger.

Rowan called and texted a thousand times a day, right up until the day I got back. I just couldn't talk to him. The messages begged me to call him. Wondering what was wrong. He even threatened to come to the island. It was the only text I allowed myself to respond to, with a "don't."

Sudden movement in the crowd near us at the base of the mountain catches my eye.

"What's wrong? You look ready to throw up," Zal says.

Quickly, I stand and mutter under my breath. "I have to go."

"What?" She jumps up.

"Stay, it's okay." My eyes shift behind her, and she follows my gaze to Rowan.

"Go. I'll stall him."

"Thank you," I manage and rush away.

With my heart beating faster, I push past a large group of people, putting distance between me and Rowan. After several more steps, I glance back. Relief floods me when I notice nobody is following me. Out of breath, I stop and suck in the cold January air.

It burns my lungs, almost immediately freezing them.

When I face forward again and take a step, I smack into someone. "Sorry," I blurt out.

"It's my fault really, for standing in your way." Rowan stares down at me.

I blink up at him. "Leave me alone, Rowan."

I try to sidestep him, but he catches my elbow, stopping me.

"You look upset. What's wrong?"

I try to pull my elbow from his grip, unsuccessfully. "You have that effect on me," I snap.

"I've had enough. This ends tonight." He tugs me by the elbow toward his motorcycle.

I dig my heels into the snow. "It ended six weeks ago."

Rowan spins so fast, I almost missed it. "You mean when you left without another word? Or when you stopped texting and calling me? What the hell is wrong with you, Jules?"

"YOU!" I shout and push his chest. "You're what's wrong with me."

Like a child, I pick up a handful of snow and throw it at him. Irrational? Yes.

But, to be fair, it's better than hitting or murdering him.

Rowan stares at me like he's seeing me for the first time. "What the hell, Jules?"

"You ruined everything," I seethe and pick up more snow, throwing it at him.

A cocky expression crosses his face as he bends down and picks up snow, throwing it back at me. "You want to fight, flannels? Game on."

As the cold, wet snow hits my face, my lips part. "I can't believe you just did that."

"You started it," he argues.

"And now, I am finishing it." I turn and walk away, but I'm suddenly tackled from behind. Rowan spins me so my back is resting on his chest, protected, when we tumble into the snow.

In the next instant, he spins us so he's pinning me to the ground, straddling me.

"Get off me."

"No! Not until you talk to me."

I stare up at him as he stares down at me. Both of us breathing hard.

After a frazzled moment, he brushes wet strands off my face. "Love the longer hair."

My mittens lift, and I try to smooth the crazy strands down. "I have to go. Let me up."

"Not until you agree to come with me for a ride," he pants.

"I believe I already agreed to do that and got burned," I snarl. "Where is my lantern?"

Understanding crosses Rowan's expression, and it changes to a slow, daring grin.

"If you keep running from me, you're never going to know what's really going on."

His comment should send me running again. But it doesn't. Instead, it piques my interest and curiosity, because Rowan Bishop knows exactly what to say, at exactly the right moment.

"What *is* going on?"

Pushing off the ground, he stands and holds out his glove-covered hand for me to take.

I stare at it.

"There is only one way to find out, flannels."

An aggravated scream builds up inside me. "You're a jerk, you know that?"

"I've been told."

His retorts only rile me up more.

Damn him.

With an angry sulk, I let him help me up. Once I'm upright, he brushes the excess snow off my legs, arms, and out of my hair. I watch him, confused by the tenderness he's showing me.

Upheaval sets in between my head and heart. The boy standing in front of me now, taking care of me, isn't connecting to the one who stole from and used me. They're too different.

He breathes in deeply, calming himself. "What is it?"

I don't answer him. I just turn and start toward the parking lot.

"Julianna, stop!"

When I don't, he lets out a low, irritated growl.

I feel the warmth of his body through my heavy coat when he presses up against my back.

"Stop," he grumbles in my ear, and all fight leaves me.

The feeling of his breath against my neck makes me close my eyes and bask in the sensation. I turn and look at him, which is a mistake, because the devastation in his expression makes me lose my breath. I try to gather my strength. I want to stay mad at him. At the situation. But all I can imagine is his lips on mine. And recall the gentle way his hands made me feel, caressing my skin.

"The Order has the lantern." His voice brings me back to reality.

"Why?" I ask dryly.

"As a precaution. In the event your family refused to let you return," he confesses.

Shock, confusion, and fear leave me standing here, bewildered. "What?"

"The lantern your grandfather gifted you, it contains a portal to Tír na nÓg, doesn't it?"

I bristle. "Yes."

"He was the gatekeeper of that portal, was he not?"

My eyes narrow. "He was."

"And when he died, he gifted you the lantern, making you the new gatekeeper."

"How do you know all this?"

"Ronan. When my brother learned of my feelings for you, and my concern about your family, it was his idea to have the Order crook and protect the lantern."

"He knows about the Order?"

"He was a member once upon a time."

I squeeze my eyes shut. My hands are balled tightly. When I open them, Rowan peers at me with apprehension. "Where is it now?"

"With an Original who is fae. Now that you're back, I will get it returned to you."

"Why not just tell me all of this, Rowan? Why all the secrets and lies?" My voice breaks.

"Because fate is mocking me," he replies. "As the daughter of a Seelie Court member, would you have handed over a realm portal that you were sworn to protect—a portal that opens to the Seelie island of Tír na nÓg —to an Unseelie fae? Even if it was for your own protection?"

I cross my arms. "You know as well as I do my oath to the Seelie Court would not have allowed me to. Regardless of my own personal feelings about you or what happened between us."

Rowan cocks his head, staying quiet.

"This isn't about our last names, it's about who we are. Seelie and Unseelie don't mix."

Something dark crosses his expression, and I immediately want to take back what I said. I didn't mean it the way it came out. "You should get home. I'll be sure the lantern is returned."

"If it gets into the wrong hands . . ." I trail off. It's not the only portal to Tír na nÓg, but it is one of very few. Any fae could have used it to realm jump. Even the Unseelie. "You've endangered the entire Seelie realm by taking it. My parents. My Court. My queen . . ." I stop.

"That's the thing about being Unseelie, Jules. I don't care who I've endangered." He backs away from me. "I only care about who I've protected."

"Rowan." I grab his coat, fear suddenly coating my throat—fear that I'll never see him again.

He leans down, his lips brushing across my ear. "I was never meant to catch you."

My breath hitches, and I'm locked in place.

He steps back and within seconds is gone.

Taking my heart with him.

SADNESS STRETCHES over me as I slide on my flannel pajama bottoms. For Christmas, I had asked for a few more pairs. Whenever I wear them now, I feel closer to Rowan. Like I'm wrapped in his warmth. I realize it sounds ridiculous and childish, but it's true. They're an extension of him.

It's been days since our snow fight. He hasn't shown up for our tutoring sessions. After two weeks, I stopped going. Stopped hoping he'd appear. I don't even care what the Court of the Sun and the Moon's punishment will be when they find out. Let them kick us out of school at this point.

I slide into bed and brush my fingers over the lantern. It showed up on my nightstand one night—no note, but Rowan's scent lingered in my bedroom, so I know he returned it.

Once again keeping his promise.

I toss and turn, sleep defying me. After about two hours, I slide out of bed and head downstairs to grab a snack. Noticing the lights are on in the family room, I walk in and see my grandmother in her elegant silk pajamas, sipping tea by the roaring fire.

"What are you doing awake, Gran?" I ask, quietly taking a seat next to her on the couch.

"Thinking of Akeel." Her eyes are trained on the fire.

"I miss him," I whisper.

"Me, too." She tilts her head so it's laying on mine. "Your grandfather had many amazing qualities, Jules, but his love and need to protect his family were what I cherished most about him."

"Protect us from what?"

"Everything." She lifts her head off mine.

"Everything meaning the Bishops?"

"Among other things," she replies and falls quiet for a bit. "Akeel would have been so disappointed by the way I handled myself and your case in front of the Court. It was a circus. And the ruling . . ." She trails off. "Forcing you and Rowan together like you are a criminal."

"Gran—" I begin, but she keeps going.

"Your grandfather and I always hoped by the time Rowan came back to Havenwood Falls, you'd already be away at college. Almost graduated, if we had our way," she admits. "And when he actually returned, I thought it was under control. Akeel should have never trusted Roman."

"What was under control? My memory? Wiping our friendship from me?" I challenge.

"Rowan told you." It's a statement of defeat, not a question.

"That this family has been drugging me for years after banishing him from Havenwood Falls, so I would forget him? Yeah. He mentioned it in passing," I reply sarcastically.

Gran shakes her head. "You two are young and naïve."

"What does that mean?"

Her eyes meet mine, then flitter away. "I can see it all over your face, Julianna. Despite this family's best efforts to protect you from the Bishop family. You are in love with him."

"And if I am? Why is that so bad?" I ask.

After a few moments of silence, she lowers her voice to a whisper. "When you were both young children, your mothers saw your connection. Against our warnings, they encouraged it. Conspiring behind everyone's backs. Hoping that one day, you and Rowan might fall in love and marry, bringing the Seelie and Unseelie fae realms together."

I sneak a peek at her. "What if Rowan and I *can* help bring two realms together?"

"Oh, Jules," she chastises. "No one wanted peace between the Seelie and Unseelie fae more than your grandfather. Your father wants it, too, which is why he agreed to take over Akeel's seat on the Court." Her eyes meet mine as she pats my hand. "Peace between the fae is not a burden you need to take on. You have your entire future to embrace. Rowan is but a fleeting moment."

"What if he's not fleeting, but fated?" I argue.

"First love is most always fleeting. Especially when it's with a Bishop."

And there it is.

No matter what is fated, or what is our choice, neither the House of Bishop nor the House of Fairchild will allow us to be together. Their ongoing feud is the real reason that Rowan was sent away. His brother didn't want him to become part of the Unseelie Court. Doing so would have meant the Bishop and Fairchild families would have been united in an attempt to secure peace and unite the fae realms. Neither family's pride would have allowed it.

I sit on the couch, quickly growing more and more irritated.

My grandmother stands and slides her palms over her pajamas, smoothing them out. "Get some rest tonight, Julianna. Tomorrow is a big birthday for you. Eighteen is a magical number."

Gran kisses my cheek and walks toward the room's entry, but before she completely leaves, I stand and face her retreating form.

"Does it even matter?" My voice is flat.

She stops, but doesn't turn to face me. "Does what matter?"

"The way *I* feel about Rowan? *My* wants and thoughts on us?"

"No."

With a flick of my wrist, the lights turn off, and the darkness settles in around me. With fae magic, I turn on my twinkle lights. I've slept with them ever since I was little. It wasn't out of fear. I've never been afraid of the dark. The lights have always calmed me, helped me relax in my sleep.

As soon as I close my eyes, a familiar empty feeling settles back in my chest. A reminder of the way I felt before Rowan came back into my life . . . like there were pieces missing. Pieces that I never could explain or understand. Until he came back and reached for my heart, putting all the pieces back. Regardless of what anyone else says, I love him. He has never given me a reason to doubt what I feel. Resolved, I grab my phone off my nightstand and shoot off a text to Zaltana.

Me: I need a favor.

Zal: Anything.

Me: I need to speak with River. The Order . . . I need their help.

Zal: Consider it done, birthday girl!

With a sigh of relief, I toss my phone onto my bed and smile. Gran was right. Eighteen is a magical number. It means I can finally make my own decisions about my life, and there isn't a darn thing the Houses of Fairchild or Bishop can do about it.

I choose Rowan.

I choose to love him.

I choose to no longer be part of this ongoing family feud.

The only thing I choose to fight for is Rowan's heart.

I know what I want. Need. Without second-guessing myself, I stand in the red dress in the middle of the Whisper Falls Inn ballroom, clutching my arrow. Rowan steps into the room, along with a few other Order members, surprisingly wearing a tuxedo and white mask.

It took River, or Achelous as he's known to the Originals, three weeks of secret meetings and planning with the society. Since I'm not a member,

I wasn't allowed to attend any of their meetings. River and I met only once, so I could tell him what I needed. He promised to come through for me. And he has.

According to Zaltana, River was able to convince the Order that for their February event, they should crash the Cupids & Cuties annual black-tie event. Attendees are given plain white masks and white arrows trimmed in gold, and then they mingle in the crowd until their arrows glow, indicating they've found their heart's true match. Then they're supposed to kiss.

Normally, you have to be eighteen or older, and half of the Originals aren't, so he leveraged it as an argument for attending—since events must be illegal or rule-breaking in some manner. I have no idea what else they have planned for tonight. No doubt, it will include something sinister. To be honest, I no longer care. All I care about is that Rowan is here. Standing a few feet away from me. Staring at me. Even though he's masked, I know it's him instantly, because power and danger emanate off him. It feels like forever since I've seen him.

The sight of him takes my breath away. My heart begins to beat wildly, stealing the air from my lungs as his gaze meets and drinks in mine. I've never experienced anything like this before, with anyone, except him. Every part of me is utterly captivated by his eyes.

Seeing him only confirms that I've never been so certain of anything in my whole life.

I walk steadily to him, stopping only when I am a breath away from his lips. His expression is guarded as his eyes track my every movement. When his gaze locks onto mine, everything else around us falls away. Swallowing, I get ready to reveal everything to him. I was tired of lying to myself. Whatever his reaction, I will deal with it, but he needs to know.

"You've been gone," I manage.

"I needed time." The words come out of his mouth in an even, unemotional way.

"Did you take the lantern to protect me? Or help your realm?" I ask him point blank.

His jaw twitches. He's annoyed with my question. "To protect you. I couldn't care less about the Unseelie and Seelie realms, or Courts," he answers truthfully.

"Do you double infinity swear?" I lift my wrist and place it on his tux, over his tattoo.

He doesn't answer, but dips his chin in agreement.

"Nothing has felt right since you walked away from me," I whisper. "I tried. Tried to be with you. Tried to not be with you. Tried to convince myself that this wasn't fated. That we aren't supposed to be together. But it won't go away. The need . . . the desire to be yours. It's too much."

He stiffens at my words.

"We're too much."

Silence falls between us as his heated stare blazes into me.

"But I love you. Regardless of your last name, or mine. In spite of your Unseelie bloodline, and what has been predestined between us. I love *you*. Not all the things that surround you."

He doesn't say anything.

"I've loved you since we were children. And just this once, if you want to, I will let you catch me," I say, my voice shaking. "Because I know once you do, you won't stop chasing me."

When he doesn't respond, I step away, but his fingers curl around my hips, pulling me back.

"We are both eighteen now, which means we control our fates and destinies. Not our families, or the fae realms. You and me. Together," I point out. "I choose to love you, Rowan."

I lift my fingers and take off his mask, and then mine. A grin swallows his lips. He bends over slowly, giving me plenty of time to object. His lips move down to mine as I become breathless and dizzy, wanting to feel them so badly, it's almost painful. With Rowan, regardless of what we will face in the future, I feel safe, protected, and happy.

He was my destiny even before he was fated to be.

"You're glowing, flannels." His voice is low and gritty.

"What?"

His hand lifts mine, and our arrows glow brightly, indicating we are a match.

"They ignite in the dark, as love awakes," he whispers.

"Does this mean I can be yours?"

He brushes his lips across mine. "You always were. And you always will be."

~

WE HOPE you enjoyed this story in the Havenwood Falls High series of novellas featuring a variety of supernatural creatures. The series is a collaborative effort by multiple authors. Each book is generally a stand-alone, so you can read them in any order, although some authors will be writing sequels to their own stories. Please be aware when you choose your next read.

Other books in the Young Adult Havenwood Falls High series:

Written in the Stars by Kallie Ross
Reawakened by Morgan Wylie
The Fall by Kristen Yard
Somewhere Within by Amy Hale
Awaken the Soul by Michele G. Miller
Bound by Shadows by Cameo Renae
Inamorata by Randi Cooley Wilson
Fata Morgana by E.J. Fechenda (March 2018)
Forever Emeline by Katie M. John (April 2018)

More books releasing on a monthly basis.

Stay up to date at www.HavenwoodFalls.com

Subscribe to our reader group and receive free stories and more!

ACKNOWLEDGMENTS

None of these stories could come to life without the love and support of my husband, Dave, and daughter, Maddison.

Kristie Cook, thank you for allowing me to debut as a YA writer for Havenwood Falls High and be part of this amazing world and group of authors. To all the authors who've allowed me to play in this world and with them and their characters, and for their ongoing collaboration, love, and support on this journey, I thank you. Special thanks to: Heather Hildenbrand, E.J. Fechenda, Lila Felix, Michele G. Miller, Belinda Boring, and Kristie Cook, for allowing me to bring your characters into this story and bring Julianna and Rowan's existence to life. A special shout-out to Michele G. Miller for sharing her love of tacos with me.

Sarah Hershman, and the team at Hershman Rights Management, thank you for your ongoing love and support. Rick and Amy Miles, and the entire Red Coat PR team, thank you for allowing me to be part of the author family. Regina Wamba at Mae I Design, thank you so much for the perfect cover, again! Liz Ferry at Per Se Editing, as always, thank you for coming into my life and polishing my stories so they shine. Pot & Kettle, thank you for capturing Julianna and Rowan's love with a beautiful song—PIECES. A HUGE thank you to Randi's Rebels. Y'all are the best reader group a girl could ask for. A very special shout out to Rebel Shae Fleming, who named River!

And to the beta readers, thank you for making Julianna and Rowan's story so much better. Thanks to my family and friends, I love you all. Thank you to the readers, for reading my stories, for continuing to take chances on me and the stories I write, and for trusting me with your imagination. As always, I'm honored to be part of your literary world.

ABOUT THE AUTHOR

Randi Cooley Wilson is a bestselling author of paranormal, urban fantasy, and contemporary romance books. Randi was born and raised in Massachusetts, where she attended Bridgewater State University and graduated with a degree in Communication Studies. After graduation, she moved to California, where she lived happily bathed in sunshine and warm weather for fifteen years.

Randi makes stuff up, devours romance books, drinks lots of wine and coffee, and has a slight addiction to bracelets. She currently resides in Massachusetts with her daughter and husband, and their fur baby, Coco Chanel.

Visit **randicooleywilson.com** for more information about Randi or her books and projects. Download the **DAMNGARGOYLE** app to keep up to date on all things Randi Cooley Wilson.

Follow Randi on the following social media outlets:

Twitter: @R_CooleyWilson
Facebook: www.facebook.com/authorrandicooleywilson
Goodreads: www.goodreads.com/RCooleyWilson
Randi's Rebels: www.facebook.com/groups/randisrebels

HAVENWOOD FALLS HIGH

Fata Morgana

E.J. FECHENDA

~ A Havenwood Falls Young Adult Novel ~

AN EXCERPT

Fata Morgana **(A Havenwood Falls High Novel) by E.J. Fechenda**

Love stinks. Love bites. Love hurts.

Paisley Underwood sings along with the countless songs about love gone wrong, but she's never experienced it for herself. With school, work, and volunteering, she doesn't have time for it. Not to mention, she's a fae on the cusp of awakening, facing unknown changes as her dominant ability emerges. When she starts her senior year at Havenwood Falls High, she has plans to make as many memories as possible with her friends. Falling in love isn't part of them.

A quiet and broody artist, Cole Silver has never been on Paisley's radar except as competition in art class. Also a fae, he went through his awakening over the summer, emerging with abilities he considers a curse. Blending in with humans had been challenging enough before, and now he's a magnet for human women. But he's inexplicably drawn to Paisley, who's thankfully not human.

When Paisley drops everything to focus all of her time and energy on Cole, her friends and family grow increasingly concerned about their unhealthy relationship. Then they discover dark secrets about Cole, his family, and his abilities, and concern morphs into a fight for Paisley's life.

Love stinks. Love bites. Love hurts. Love can be a lie.

FATA MORGANA

AN EXCERPT

COLE

One second made the difference between life and death. Had I been paying closer attention, I could have avoided disaster. Gwen, the owner of Tragic Ink, where I had been hanging out as an apprentice, had finally let me do my own ink, and I was distracted as I left the studio, watching how the natural light played off of the deep blues on my new tattoo. When I stepped onto the sidewalk, I didn't see the human girl coming at me, and we collided. She practically bounced off of me. Reflexes kicked in, and without thinking, I reached out to steady her. The moment my hands touched her bare upper arms, I realized my mistake. I quickly pulled away, but it was too late. The girl's pupils dilated, and her dreamy gaze fixated on me. She was hooked that quickly and already doomed.

Just one touch from me was like being marked by a reaper.

"Hi," she said breathlessly, tucking a stray blond hair behind her ear as she batted her eyelashes. "I'm Emily."

She took a step closer to me, and I took a step back, hoping to keep some distance between us, but the girl eyed me like she was a lioness and I was her prey. The same look I'd seen in another girl's eyes in Colorado Springs earlier this summer. A girl I'd kissed and was now dead. Emily licked her lips and grabbed my hand, not knowing she was already an addict, desperate for her next fix.

Here we were in the middle of town on a warm summer evening, where there were too many witnesses.

How quickly the excitement over doing my own tattoo faded. It had taken me close to three hours as I methodically and painstakingly applied the needle to my pale skin. There was a large probability of error doing work on myself, and I hadn't wanted to screw up. The end result was exactly how I envisioned it—the beginning of a much bigger design that would eventually be a full sleeve.

Even Gwen was impressed and told me I did a good job. Since she barely interacted with me except to tell me when something needed to be cleaned, or to send me on a coffee run to Broastful Brew, I knew that was something. I wanted to be a tattoo artist and own a studio someday, and this experience just bolstered my dream, especially after the nightmare my summer had been so far. And that nightmare was far from over.

I hated what I had become after my awakening, and I was still trying to learn to control my abilities. Of course, I would be the one to inherit a long-dormant gene, passed down through generations. Gancanagh were a rare species of Greater Fae, but there was nothing great about being a gancanagh. It was a curse. My looks were transformed, making me irresistible to human women, but a single touch from me meant certain death. When they came in contact with my skin, the toxin I secreted was more addictive than the most potent heroin and crack combined. And more deadly.

"What's your name?" Emily asked, breaking the thoughts bouncing around in my head. I realized she still had a hold of my hand. Her cheeks were flushed, her blue eyes bright with lust, and she literally buzzed as my toxin coursed through her veins. How was I going to explain to my parents that it had happened again, but this time in Havenwood Falls —our home?

"Listen, I'm sorry for running into you, but I gotta go." Like a coward, I planned on bolting.

I didn't recognize this girl and wondered if she was one of the many tourists visiting Havenwood Falls. Would she be gone before the symptoms kicked in, completely unaware that her time on earth was drawing to an end? I started to extract my hand from her grip, but she stepped forward again, pressing her body against mine. That's when her energy hit me, and my body started to hum from the infusion. I could drain her dry, right here on the sidewalk, and leave her a weak shell until she wasted away, but that was cruel. That was the mindset of a monster —not me.

She was younger than me, but only by a year or two, making her sixteen or seventeen. I was sure I would have known her if she lived here. Emily's other hand slipped into the back pocket of my jeans, and she tugged me closer. She tilted her head up to look at me. Her eyes were dark, completely dilated. Her cheeks were flushed like she was running a fever. Her mouth parted, and she licked her lips. At this point, the roles reversed, and I found her irresistible. Energy, her very life essence, poured off of her, and the need to absorb it took over. Any resistance, any efforts to control myself were lost, and I was weakened by the temptation. Leaning down, I captured her lips with mine, sealing her fate.

~

PAISLEY

My friends and I stopped our giggling the moment my bedroom door creaked open. I fully expected my brother, Dalton, to be there, ready to shoot us with his Nerf gun again, but my mom's face appeared instead.

"Hi, girls, I'm going to make some cookies and will bring them up when they're done."

This was received with a couple of excited squeals.

"Thanks!" my cousin Julianna called out.

The moment the door closed, the giggling continued. We were talking about boys and who we were excited to see when school started in two weeks.

"He's only going to be a junior, but Will Kasun is fine. Oh, and Logan is huge. He could bench press me any day," Makenna, my best friend, said. Her cheeks turned bright red before she buried her face in a pillow. She was a cheerleader and spent most of her time stalking from afar during cheer practice.

"Yeah, but Logan is so in love with Serena. She just doesn't see it," Zal said, and Julianna murmured in agreement, unusually quiet and not contributing to the conversation.

"What about you, Paisley? Who are you looking forward to seeing?" Zal asked, breaking the silence and steering the conversation back to a lighter topic.

I tilted my head slightly as I thought about my answer. No particular guy came to mind. "I don't know. Honestly, between work, volunteering at the medical center, and getting everything together for the pageant, I haven't had time to think about anything else."

"Oh, the pageant! Who do you think will be Miss Teen Havenwood Falls this year—do you think you'll win?" Makenna was easily distracted and seized on the new topic like a cat pouncing on a red laser dot.

"I don't care if I win. My mom and Willow basically forced me to enter because it's family tradition." I met Julianna's gaze from across the room. It was like staring into my own, as we had the same shade of violet eyes.

While I had been the one to convince Julianna to enter the pageant with me, I knew she would win. I mean, she excelled in everything. She smiled at me before turning her attention to Zal, her best friend. Physically, those two were polar opposites. Like me, Julianna had fair, almost luminescent skin and where I had purple highlights, Julianna's hair was naturally lavender. Zaltana had dark skin and hair as black as ink. She was the granddaughter of the chief of local band of the Ute tribe, and she looked every bit Native American royalty.

Talking about the coming school year and the pageant made me feel suddenly anxious, and with a dramatic sigh, I fell back against a pile of pillows stacked against my headboard. As if I didn't have enough to worry about between figuring out what to do after high school and the uncertainty of when I was going to go through my awakening, the pageant was an annoyance I could do without.

I was turning eighteen in May, less than a year away, and knew my awakening could happen at any time. Makenna and Julianna, who were both fae, had already gone through theirs. Makenna had to take a week off of school until she learned how to control her abilities. My cousin Willow told me that when she went through her awakening, her emotions were off the chart, like PMS on meth. She'd told me her story a million times, but it never grew old. It was part of Havenwood Falls history. Willow didn't know at the time that she was coming into her full powers as an empath, and had she known what was going on, she might have been able to prevent the Vampire Massacre of 2005.

I tuned out my friends as the conversation returned to boys. All summer, I'd been obsessed with wondering what my dominant ability would be once I went through my awakening. Would I be a bomb-ass gardener like my mom, who could make any plant grow in the most extreme conditions? Would I inherit my dad's healing abilities, which made him one of the more popular doctors at the medical center? Maybe I'd be an empath like my cousin Willow? Who knew what fate had in store for me? I couldn't wait to find out, but was nervous, too. This year was going to bring a lot of change.

I looked around the room at my friends, who were sitting in a circle on the floor in the middle of my room. Taylor had brought a Ouija board and was setting it up. She was the only one out of this group who attended the Sun and Moon Academy. Makenna, with her red hair that reminded me so much of Aster, my former manager at Coffee Haven, grinned at me when my gaze landed on her.

"Get your butt down here, Underwood," she said and patted the empty space next to her. "We're going to conjure up some spirits. Maybe we can call up a smoking hot ghost. Has anyone dated a ghost?"

I eyed the Ouija board uneasily because, knowing Taylor's power, we were going to be bringing a spirit forth. At least she was a competent medium, and I knew she'd be able to send them back. We didn't Ouija irresponsibly. Taylor was a member of the Luna Coven, and they would come down on her hard if she misused her magic.

Later that night, with our bellies full of cookies and milk, we lay down, getting comfortable. I yawned and turned onto my back, staring at the ceiling. I had strung tiny white lights up all around the room, where the walls and ceiling met. These, combined with the silvery, watery light that spilled in from the moon outside, cast my room in a soft, dreamy glow. The house was quiet. Dalton had given up trying to scare us, and my parents had gone to bed. Makenna sighed and rolled toward me. We were sharing my bed while Julianna, Zal, and Taylor were stretched out on the floor with yoga mats and sleeping bags.

"Can you believe we're going to be seniors?" she asked.

"Technically we already are, but I know what you mean. It seems like yesterday we were starting middle school."

"Do you guys remember how nervous we were about being freshmen?" Taylor asked. "I like seriously almost threw up in the bushes by the front steps of the Academy. The seniors then seemed so mature, ya know?"

"It went by so fast. Let's make this the best year ever. Promise?" I said, rolling to face Makenna. "Who knows where we're all going to be this time next year."

Makenna reached for my hand, and we linked pinkies. We had been making pinky swears since we were seven, taking them as seriously as any vow or oath.

After everyone else fell asleep, I lay awake listening to their soft breathing. *How many more sleepovers are we going to have?* We all had decisions to make about our future. Some of us were going to leave Havenwood Falls and never come back, our childhood memories wiped away. Some of us would stay, but adulthood would mold us into different people. We'd be burdened with more responsibility. I linked my pinky with Makenna's again, and she mumbled in her sleep, but didn't wake. I wished we could stay like this forever, that my room could become an impenetrable bubble keeping my friends and me safe from outside forces. With that final thought, I finally drifted off to sleep, blissfully unaware of how quickly things were going to change.

Made in the USA
Monee, IL
08 December 2024